Melange

Melange

Kristy Tate

Indie Artist Press | *Brackettville, Texas*

Melange
A novel by Kristy Tate
First Paperback Edition
Copyright © Kristy Tate 2018
All Rights Reserved
Printed in the United States of America
ISBN-13:978-1-62522-129-2

Publisher Information-
Indie Artist Press
P. O. Box 131
Brackettville, TX 78832
www.indieartistpress.com

Coyote is always
out there waiting, and
Coyote is always hungry.
~Navajo

Chapter One

On the sort of spring evening that lasts forever, when the sun's fading into blackness stretches for hours, Declan tried to convince himself that time really could be harnessed, and the simple pleasure he found walking beside Lizbet and listening to her laugh would last as long as they both lived. And yet his errand reminded him that bits and pieces of life could be fleeting, that nothing lasts forever, and things could change as quickly as the weather. But fortunately, at that moment, the finicky Pacific Northwest sky sported a few wispy clouds and a promise of a cool, clear night.

"Are you sure you want to wait?" Declan asked.

"What else am I going to do?" Lizbet asked. "Besides, hanging in a bookstore is one of my favorite things to do."

"I feel weird having you walk me to my grandfather's house." He skated a glance at her, wondering what his grandfather would think of Lizbet's curly hair, elfin features, tiny build, and bright green eyes. His mom called Lizbet a wild child, which was, given her strange upbringing, an apt description. "It's supposed to go the other way, right?"

"What do you mean?" Lizbet turned to him.

He wanted to kiss her, but after a quick peek at his grandfather's imposing brick mansion on the other side of the long stretch of lawn beyond the wrought-iron gate, he tucked his hands into his pockets to stop himself from reaching out to her. "I'm the guy," he said. "I'm supposed to walk you home."

"But neither of us are going home. I'm going to the bookstore, and you're stalling."

"I'm not stalling."

She placed her hands on his chest to keep him away. "Yes, you are. We've been walking down this street at turtle speed..."

He wrapped his hands around her wrists, holding her close. "He's going to think I'm hitting him up for money."

"Why do you say that?"

Declan sucked in a breath. "He's going to ask about college, so I'll have to tell him about Duke, and that will lead to a conversation about money."

"If I were you, I'd rather talk about money than your stepfather."

"True that." Declan didn't like to think of, let alone speak about, his stepfather. Fortunately for him, although unfortunately for his stepfather's business, Gaylord Godwin had been missing for weeks.

"But you're not your stepfather, and you don't have to talk about money. You can steer the conversation in any direction you wish."

A rustling in the bushes caught Declan's attention. The giant rhododendrons bordering the lawn shivered before falling still.

Lizbet followed his gaze, her expression curious and baffled.

"Probably a cat," Declan said.

Lizbet shook herself and tucked her hands into her sweater pockets. "I don't think so... It would have been a really big cat."

"A dog then," Declan said, dismissing it. "Are you going to be okay walking to the bookstore?"

Lizbet smirked. "I don't know... This is a pretty sketchy neighborhood." She waved at the turn-of-the-last-century mansions, tree-lined street, and manicured lawns before taking his hand in hers and squeezing it. "Visiting your grandfather is the kind thing to do. Remember, this is for him, not you. I'll be fine and so will you. And more importantly, so will your grandfather."

But Declan knew that wasn't true. The whole reason he stood on the street outside his grandfather's house was

because the old man wasn't fine. His days were numbered. According to his nurse, Frank Forsythe only continued to live because he was too ornery to die.

"He scares me," Declan admitted.

"I think you could take him on," Lizbet said with a grin.

"Physically, but probably not intellectually."

"If he tries to play chess, just run." Lizbet put her hands on Declan's shoulders and turned him so he faced the front gate.

"That would be cowardly..." Declan shuffled his feet.

Lizbet gave his back a gentle push.

The bushes shook again and this time Declan caught sight of an enormous gray tail beating the bright red flowers before disappearing into the shrubs. "That's a huge dog."

"I'm not scared of a dog," Lizbet assured him.

"What if my grandfather gets talking and I can't get away before the bookstore closes? I can't leave you in the dark by yourself while a giant dog runs loose, terrorizing the neighborhood." Declan balked at the black wrought-iron gate that separated his grandfather's house from the rest of the world.

"For one thing, no one is terrorized. And another, this is the Pacific Northwest. It's June, the longest day of the year is only a few weeks away. We have another two hours, at least, of daylight. And if your grandfather gets extra chatty, I'll take a bus home." She reached around him and pushed open the gate. "Now, march up to that door and act chummy. He's old, he's sick, and he wants to meet you."

Declan nodded and, after a quick backward glance at Lizbet, the girl who had become the center of his world, headed up the walkway.

As much as the bookstore tempted Lizbet, curiosity made her pause at the edge of Frank Forsythe's property near the now-still rhododendrons. Cocking her head, she listened for the dog that belonged to the great furry tail she'd spotted earlier. She shot Declan a quick peep. He stood on the porch with his hands shoved into his pockets, his back to her.

"Hello?" Lizbet whispered into the bushes. Silence. She scanned the trees lining the property, expecting to catch the attention of a squirrel or even a bird, but couldn't find a creature in sight. A chill crawled down her back. "Hello?" she called a smidge louder.

The bushes rustled again and Lizbet searched for the cause. A rabbit, a chipmunk, even a skunk—there had to be an animal around. Why wasn't anyone responding? She gave the house another glance, but Declan had disappeared from the porch.

She hadn't heard the front door open, but that must have been what had happened. The nurse, Teddy, had been expecting him. Lizbet let out a little sigh of relief, pulled her sweater a bit tighter, and headed for the Blarney Bookstore.

The University District was an eclectic mix of shops

catering to the UW's students, and the historic homes of the professors and Seattle's business professionals. Lizbet's sandals made a flopping sound as she walked and she told herself that the eerie echo wasn't in any way sinister. But goosebumps rose on her skin as she scanned the yards, trees, and shrubbery for signs of life.

Where was everyone? The only reason she knew for the animals to desert an area was a forest fire, and the warm humidity held only a spark of the imagination. Unfortunately, Lizbet's imagination was running wild. She tried to rein it in as she headed for the bookstore.

When only silence answered the door, Declan had stepped off the porch to peek in the window. He'd never been inside his grandfather's house, so he didn't know what to expect. The Oriental rugs, wingback chairs, and pastoral paintings didn't surprise him. The overturned table, shattered vase, and flowers strewn across the wood floor did. He rapped on the window. Just like when he'd knocked on the door, no one answered.

He cast another look around for Lizbet and spotted her at the intersection at the end of the street. Should he call out to her? What if someone had broken into his grandfather's home? What if that someone was still in the house? The farther away Lizbet was, the safer she was. Squaring his shoulders and refusing to jump to conclusions, Declan

jogged toward the back of the house. A shoulder-high brick wall enclosed the backyard. When he couldn't find a gate, he scrambled over the wall and landed hard on his feet. His breathing accelerated as he picked up his pace. A quick peek in the windows told him the living and dining room were both empty. A motion–sensor light flicked on when he reached the patio. Everything in the backyard screamed quiet and peaceful elegance. It was hard to imagine his grandfather had met any violence. The windows were intact, but the back door hung ajar.

Declan reached into his pocket and fingered his phone, debating whether he should call the police. He poked his head through the door. The kitchen with its tall white cabinetry, scrubbed oak table, and gleaming stainless-steel appliances looked like it belonged in a magazine. But a large butcher knife lay on the floor, surrounded by a smattering of... What was that?

Declan pushed inside for a better look, then, with trembling fingers, he called his mom.

Lizbet finally spotted an owl perched on a branch of a giant maple tree. It was early for an owl, but that was only one of the things out of place on this strange evening. Lizbet glanced up and down the street, making sure that she and the owl were alone. "Where is everyone?" she asked.

The owl swiveled his head in her direction and blinked

at her. *"The wolves have returned,"* he said with a hoot, as if this should answer all her questions.

"The wolves? In the University District?" Her mind tripped back to the large gray tail she'd spotted in Frank Forsythe's rhododendrons. Why would there be wolves close to the city center? Wolves belonged in the woods or near pastures where the slow and easy prey lived.

The owl blinked again and nodded.

"All the animals have disappeared because of the wolves?" Lizbet pressed.

"I suggest you do the same."

"Why are you here?"

"I am a sentinel. We owls have always been so."

"Admirable," Lizbet murmured. She pressed her mouth closed when an elderly couple walking a Standard Poodle appeared at the end of the street. She watched as the poodle sat down and refused to budge. The woman tugged on the leash and reprimanded the stubborn dog. After a moment, the man took the lead, but the dog remained obstinate. The man pulled, but the poodle sat on his haunches while his collar threatened to pop off his furry head.

She turned back to the owl. "Do you know where the wolves are now?"

The owl lifted one wing and pointed at the Forsythe house.

Lizbet ran and her sandals slapped the sidewalk.

She stopped short when a giant gray wolf appeared on the sidewalk. His solid muscles rippled beneath silvery fur.

His broad shoulders were powerful and his flanks sturdy. He lowered his head and emitted a low growl. "What...who are you?" she asked the wolf.

He didn't answer but stared at her with blazing green eyes. It occurred to Lizbet that he was trying to scare her. She balled her fists and planted them on her hips. "Answer me!" She raised her voice and tried to infuse it with authority. "Who are you and what do you want?"

The creature flicked his tail before turning and sauntering into the shadowy twilight. She stared after him for half a second before opening the wrought-iron gate, rushing down the walkway, climbing the steps to the front porch, and rapping on the door.

Declan answered, his face pale. Silently, he widened the door to let her in. "I thought you were the police." His voice wavered.

"Why? What happened?"

Declan nodded over his shoulder. A newscaster's voice floated through an open door and light flickered from a TV screen in a room off the hall.

Lizbet started for it, but Declan put a warning hand on her arm, stopping her. "Don't," he said.

"Why?"

"Well, for one thing, I vomited in there. And another..."

"Your grandfather?"

"And Teddy, his nurse."

"Are they dead?" Lizbet whispered, although she didn't know why.

"It's... grizzly."

Lizbet put her fingers to her lips, because she knew it wasn't grizzly—not like a bear—but wolfish, like a giant gray wolf.

Every animal knows
more than you do.
~Nez Perce

Chapter Two

After several hours with the police, Lizbet finally arrived back at her grandmother's ranch. She tested the locks on all the gates and fences, and checked in with the animals. She didn't mention the wolves because she knew how skittish the horses could be and how it was really easy to send the chickens into a panic. She tried to sound casually conversational as she chatted with the goats and a passing rabbit.

Gazing up at the sky, she thought about calling to a circling owl. The birds were always the first in the know, but since it was a warm evening without a promise of rain she knew her mom and grandmother would have their windows open, and she didn't want to alarm them any more than the chickens.

Her mother's window shone with a soft warm light, letting her know that Daugherty was still awake and probably waiting for her. Lizbet's heart lifted. It had only been a few weeks since her mother had woken from her coma, and Lizbet still felt profound gratitude for her mother, even though sometimes she felt that her mom was a different person here at the ranch than she'd been on the island where Lizbet had grown up. Still, Daugherty was her rock— the only permanent thing in Lizbet's life. She hurried inside to tell her mother about Declan's grandfather.

Daugherty sat on the edge of her bed. The shell-shocked expression on her face told Lizbet that her mom had already heard the news. Daugherty held out her arms in a greeting when she caught sight of Lizbet.

"Did you see him?" Daugherty asked after Lizbet dropped into her mother's arms.

Lizbet inhaled her mom's familiar scent of vanilla and honey and shook her head. "Declan did."

"Oh, that poor guy." Daugherty stroked Lizbet's curls.

"He was pretty shaken. He vomited." Lizbet pulled away and sat beside her mom. The mattress shifted, sliding them together so their shoulders and thighs met.

Daugherty patted Lizbet's leg. "John told me."

Lizbet met her mom's gaze and smiled. "He's not still mad then?"

"Oh, he's still mad."

"But not too mad to talk to you?"

Daugherty studied the floor and shook her head.

"He'll come around. He loves you."

"He loved me when he thought I was a fantasy, but now that he knows I'm real..."

Lizbet softly laughed. "This is the downside of ginger root tea."

"We can't blame the tea."

But Lizbet had some hard feelings of her own about the tea her mom had used to cause a forgetfulness almost as deep as Daugherty's own amnesia. Lizbet knew she and her mom were lucky to be able to live with Elizabeth, Lizbet's grandmother, while Daugherty tried to recreate their lives after a nearly twenty-year solitary hiatus on Blackstone Island. John, Declan's dad, had been the only person to visit them who actually knew Daugherty, but thanks to the tea, John had thought she was nothing more than a hallucination. And he hadn't ever even seen Lizbet until they had met on the mainland after Daugherty's hospitalization.

"What do you think will happen now?" Lizbet asked.

"You mean for Declan?" Daugherty asked. "Well, according to John, he's not a suspect, even though often the person to discover a body is."

"Why not?"

"The vomit, for one thing, but also the nature of the wounds."

Lizbet sucked in a deep breath. "So weird, right? Who ever heard of wolves in the center of Queen Anne?"

Daugherty nodded and slid a look at Lizbet. "Do you know anything about wolves?"

"Only what I read in *My Antonia*." For a reason she couldn't define, Lizbet had kept her ability to talk with animals a carefully guarded secret. She'd learned long ago that her mother couldn't hear or understand the animals the way Lizbet did. At first, this had bothered Lizbet. For years, she had believed her mother to be all-knowing and all-powerful, but in time, Lizbet had grown to love that she had an ability her mother not only didn't share but also discounted as a childish whim akin to make-believe friends and monsters beneath the bed.

The cellphone on the nightstand buzzed. Lizbet and her mom just stared at it. Josie, Daugherty's sister and Lizbet's aunt, had given Daugherty the phone so she could keep a constant line of communication open with Lizbet's aging grandmother.

Lizbet peeked at the screen. "It's John."

"I know."

Lizbet nudged her mom's arm. "You should answer it."

Daugherty sighed. "Everything was so much easier on the island."

"No, it wasn't. Don't glamourize it." She rested her hand on her mom's thigh. "It was also a lot of hard work."

"I know, but with John..."

"The best is yet to be." Lizbet finished her mom's sentence.

"Do you really think so? Do you think he's ever going to forgive me?"

"Don't you think he might be a tiny bit mad at himself? I mean, he's the one who got snookered with ginger root tea."

"But I'm the one who gave it to him!"

"So what? That's like blaming the arms dealer for a shooter's rampage." Lizbet paused, then added softly, "Besides, you can't be held responsible. You had amnesia. You didn't know who John was. You didn't even know who you were!" Lizbet thought about bringing up Rose, her biological mother, but decided to wait for a better time. She bottled up her curiosity and put a cork in it. "Did John say how Declan's mom is doing?"

"Gloria is frantic. She's afraid the police are going to try and pin the murder on her missing husband." Only a few weeks ago, Declan's stepfather—and possibly Lizbet's real father—had left Daugherty for dead and later had taken a few potshots at Lizbet as well. Since then, he had disappeared.

"I don't know how Gloria can still care about him."

Daugherty shrugged. "Love is complicated."

Lizbet thought about her relationships with her mom, Declan, Maria, Elizabeth, even Matias. The word complicated didn't even come close to describing them.

"Besides," her mother continued, "Frank Forsythe wasn't killed by a man. They suspect he died of a heart attack."

"And what about the nurse?"

"He died from the wounds and blood loss. There's no way of knowing if a person was or wasn't responsible for the animal attack. No sign of forced entry."

"Then we might never know," Lizbet said, but what she thought was, *I'm going to find the beast, whether human or wolf, responsible for this.*

Declan tried not to be embarrassed for his mom as she fluttered around the gravesite, acting more like she was hosting an open house for a swanky townhome than grieving for her father in a coffin. She had told Declan that the service would be limited to family and a few close friends, but he felt small and lost in the sea of people surrounding his grandfather's grave. It bugged him that most of these people probably knew his grandfather better than he did. He blamed his mom. She and her dad hadn't spoken in years. Declan had never been able to cross the chasm between them.

He peeked over his shoulder at the hospitality van parked next to the small chapel adjacent to the graveyard. Even from a distance he recognized Mr. Croft and Missy, the caterers his mom always used for open houses and other events. He had suggested that she use Lizbet's mom. Daugherty was trying to get a catering business off the ground and had thrown a few luncheons and business events for family and friends using her unique blends of food and wine, but Gloria had been adamant about hiring Mr. Croft.

Which was fine... he supposed. He liked Mr. Croft.

He just liked Lizbet and her mom more. His dad, John, hovered in the back. Declan felt his dad watching him and turned, catching his eye. His big shoulders filled out his suit, and the tie looked like a noose around his neck. Knowing his dad hadn't liked Frank Forsythe any more than Gloria had, Declan guessed that John was only here for him. He also figured Gloria, who was whispering in the ear of a city councilman, wouldn't miss him, so he headed toward his dad.

Feeling like a fish trying to swim upstream, Declan weaved through the crowd. A hand on his arm stopped him. Seconds later, he was engulfed in a tight hug.

"OMG, I'm so sad for you!" Nicole breathed into his ear.

He pulled away and straightened his tie. "I didn't know him. We never even met."

"And that makes it so much more tragical."

Tragical? He'd never known Nicole to make up words. With her pale skin and hair, light blue eyes, and plain black dress, she was the opposite of Lizbet in almost every way. The sun's rays glinted off the silver cross around her neck, making him blink.

"If you need to talk, I lost my grandma a few months ago, so I know what it's like."

Since Nicole's grandma had probably died peacefully in a hospital bed rather than being ripped to pieces by a wolf, Nicole did not know how he was feeling. He couldn't tell her that the sight of his grandfather's bloody and torn

body haunted him. He couldn't tell her that the rusty smell of blood and putrid stink of death clung to him like a mold he couldn't wash away. He couldn't admit to her, or anyone, that a gray wolf with emerald eyes lived in his nightmares.

"Who's that?" Nicole asked.

Declan followed her gaze to the gravesite where a tall man with honey-blond hair stood beside his mom. "I'm not sure." It could have been any one of his grandfather's 'family and close friends,' but something about the man's posture leaning toward his mom told him that this wasn't just anyone. Declan tightened his lips and threw his dad another glance. Fortunately, John was involved in a hushed conversation with East End High's science teacher. Declan thought he caught the word *quarterback*.

Nicole elbowed him. "Your mom wants you," she whispered.

His mom waved him over with her white handkerchief. The crowd parted as he headed her way.

"Darling." Gloria reached out and placed her hand on his arm. "This is Leo Cabriolet."

"Godwin's tennis partner," Declan said. Recognizing the name, he took the man's extended hand in a firm grip.

"Former partner," Cabriolet said.

"Also your grandfather's attorney," Gloria said.

Declan studied his mom and read her excitement. He felt ill and off balance. He blamed the sun, lack of sleep, and his nightmares.

"We need to talk," Cabriolet said.

"Of course," Gloria said, looking like she was ready to find a comfortable tombstone to settle down on for a long chat.

Declan glanced around at the crowd and shook his head. "This isn't the best time."

Cabriolet nodded. "Tomorrow then?"

For some reason, Declan wanted to say he had school, basketball practice, or work, but since the next day was Sunday, he said none of those things.

"Ten?" Gloria suggested.

Cabriolet smiled. "I look forward to it." He cuffed Declan's arm in a friendly goodbye, as if they were meeting for a date instead of the reading of a will.

Lizbet watched her mom and grandmother move to the front of the crowd while she hung back in the shade of a giant maple tree. Above her, a squirrel chattered, but she paid him little attention.

Large groups of people made her nervous. It still took her by surprise that this was exactly where her mother belonged—this was the world where Daugherty had been raised. These well-dressed, diamond-flashing peers of Declan's grandfather had been the parents of her mother's playmates.

Lizbet smiled, watching her grandmother. Elizabeth

didn't ooze money as the others did, but even in her last-century dress, heels, and hose, she belonged. Her husband's wealth and land holdings had secured his wife and daughter's position on East End's slippery social ladder.

Lizbet sought out Declan. She spotted him near the gravesite, hovering near his mom and Nicole. Nicole whispered something in his ear, and he turned and gave her a brief smile. Lizbet's heart tightened as if someone had tied a string around it. She knew Declan planned on leaving in a few months. He and Nicole both planned on attending Duke University. Lizbet wondered who had made their plan first.

She didn't hold Declan's leash. She wanted him to go to the *best* school that could *best* prepare him for the *best* med school. He deserved the best. But she also knew that what was necessarily best for him might not be best for her. The thought of him leaving while she stayed behind made her ache.

Her own plans were nebulous. Her mom and grandmother wanted her to go to school. She wanted that, too. Maybe. She didn't know. She'd never been to school. It intimidated her and she had no idea what she wanted to study... or do after graduation. Besides, she really wanted to stay and help her grandmother on the ranch, and Daugherty was attempting to start a business, so that was also interesting. Lizbet had decided to attend a local community college that would allow her to keep her job

at the nursery, live on the ranch with her grandmother and mom, and lend her mom the occasional hand with the fledgling business. She tried to be content with this plan, but adventures in foreign lands tempted her. Duke University, even though she knew she'd never be accepted, also tempted her. But only because Declan would be there... and so would Nicole.

John pulled away from a group of middle-aged men. With his football player build, thick brown hair, and strong jaw, he looked too young to be Declan's father. He took Elizabeth's arm and helped her find a seat beneath the white hospitality tent. Lizbet strained to hear what he said to Daugherty.

She understood why he was mad. She just hoped he would get over it soon. What her mom had done was wrong—no one deserved to be doped up on ginger root tea—but Lizbet couldn't hold her mother accountable for what she'd done while suffering from memory loss. Then again, Lizbet had read that amnesiacs, as well as those under a hypnotic spell, would never do anything that went against their personal code of morals and ethics. Which made her wonder where ginger root tea fell into her mother's moral compass.

Lizbet guessed John had the same concerns as she watched him and her mom exchange a few brief words. Even from a distance, Lizbet could see mutual attraction buzzing between them like an electric current.

She hugged herself, feeling, as she often did, misplaced. Someone nudged her. Turning, she smiled up at Declan's enormous best friend, Baxter Dresden. His suit pants looked a little short and his jacket was too tight, but she was glad to see him.

"Hey," he said. "Does Declan know you're here?"

Lizbet shook her head. "It's okay. He should be with his family, especially his mom."

She watched Declan's face as he talked with Nicole.

"You should at least let him know you're here." Something in Baxter's tone made her wonder how he felt about Nicole.

Lizbet shrugged.

"Finding the right someone is like finding a pair of shoes," Baxter said.

"What does that mean?" Lizbet asked, smiling up at him. Declan had told her that both of Baxter's parents were therapists, and he frequently quoted them.

"It means that people look for good-looking, smart shoes, but they always end up with the ones they feel the most comfortable with."

Lizbet didn't know if Baxter was comparing her to a pair of broken-in loafers, but as he waved Declan over, she decided not to take offense when she was pretty sure none was intended.

Relief washed over Declan's face when he caught sight of Lizbet. Immediately, he broke off his conversation with Nicole and headed for Lizbet. She decided she'd be loafers, stilettos, or gumboots—any footwear Declan

desired—as long as he always looked at her this way.

Bile rose in Declan's throat when he entered his grandfather's house. The memory of his last visit flashed in his mind no matter how hard he tried to oust it. His mom had told him that professional cleaners had scoured and steamed, but... was it his imagination or did the stench of death still hang in the air? He didn't have a reference point. He had no idea how his grandfather's house had smelled before the wolf—or possibly wolves. Pipe tobacco odor puffed up from the upholstered sofa when Declan took a seat.

"I hope you don't mind meeting here," Leo Cabriolet said as he settled into a wingback chair directly opposite Declan and his mom. "It seemed easier."

For whom? Declan wondered.

Cabriolet set his briefcase on the coffee table between them. He pulled out an inch-thick document and placed it before Gloria. "This is an overview of your father's financials."

Gloria perched on the edge of the sofa. Her excitement radiated toward Declan, smothering him. She picked up the papers with shaky hands.

Cabriolet leaned back and crossed one ankle over the other. "I'm sure you'll have questions. It's a lot to process. As you know, your father had numerous investments and properties. Holbrook St. James, your grandfather's

accountant, will want to meet with you as soon as possible."

"Of course," Gloria murmured.

Cabriolet cleared his throat. "I hate to be indelicate, but..."

"You're wondering about Godwin," Gloria said without looking up from the financial statements.

"Have you heard from him?" Cabriolet asked.

Gloria locked her eyes with his. Something passed between them, but Declan couldn't decipher it.

She shook her head. "He can't think that he can take potshots at my son and still be welcome in my life!"

"Men like Godwin consider themselves welcome wherever they wish to be."

Gloria bristled. "He is totally irrelevant to me, my son, and this." She shook the papers at Cabriolet.

Cabriolet leaned forward and placed his elbows on his knees. "You may feel that way, but it's not necessarily accurate. As I'm sure you are aware, Washington is a community property state. This means that all income earned and property acquired by either spouse during the marriage is considered joint property."

Gloria stood. "But that can't be true of my inheritance!"

Cabriolet eyed her. "I'm afraid so."

Gloria sank back onto the sofa and a puff of pipe tobacco filled the air. "Is there nothing I can do? I'll divorce him this minute!"

"Divorce proceedings can take time," Cabriolet said. "Especially if you don't know where one of the party is."

"I've heard of people going to Idaho for a quickie divorce," Gloria murmured.

"He would still need to sign the papers."

Gloria bounced back to her feet and began to pace. "I need to find him!"

"Mom, the police are looking for him," Declan said. "I'm sure they'll find him. And even if they don't, that's good, right? He can't claim anything if he's hiding."

Gloria ran her hand over the heavily carved fireplace mantel. "I'm going to move in here."

"What?" Declan asked, feeling slightly dizzy.

"My father was paranoid." Gloria's attention flashed around the room as if she were searching for hidden cameras. "I bet he has a topnotch security system."

Declan thought about pointing out that it hadn't done him much good. "Your house also has a security system."

"But Godwin knows the passwords."

"Then change them," Declan put in.

Gloria shook her head. "Don't you see? His name is also on the account. He could change it at any time. No, this will be better."

"You're making the right decision," Cabriolet said. "You'll be safer here."

It hadn't been such a safe place for Declan's grandfather. He thought his mom should realize this, but he didn't want to be the one to tell her.

"Should I call the security company now?" Gloria stood before Cabriolet.

"No. Just lock the doors behind us. I'm sure you'll be fine until tomorrow."

Gloria nodded, but bit her lip and looked unsure. "Will you come with me to speak to St. James?"

Cabriolet flushed and looked pleased. "If you wish."

The undercurrent between them grew thicker and murkier, and Declan's sensation of being smothered washed over him again.

The following Friday, Lizbet stood on the steps of East End High. Walking through the doors was like crossing the border into a foreign territory. The long halls lined with banks of lockers, the posters on the classrooms' windows and doors, the student-painted murals on the walls—this was an alien nation. She didn't know the language or customs. She could never learn their mores in books. It bothered her that this was Declan's world and it was one she'd never understand.

She shook away her self-doubts and tried to match her mom's hurried pace. Laden with donut boxes, Daugherty strode down the hall as if she knew exactly where she was headed. Lizbet realized with a start that of course Daugherty knew the way to the home ec room—East End High was also her alma mater.

"We only have a couple of hours after the ceremony to set up for grad night." Daugherty pushed open the home ec room door and placed the stack of donut boxes on the countertop. The boxes, purchased from Dee's Delights, the local bakery, were not filled with donuts, but nearly a thousand cookies all baked by Daugherty, Lizbet, and Elizabeth. Half were of the more traditional flavors, such as chocolate chip and sugar, but Lizbet's favorite was Daugherty's own creation, the blackberry bongo bar.

The senior grad night was Daugherty's largest gig to date. Declan's dad, who was East End's head football coach, had set it up for her. Lizbet knew that none of the East End seniors would be repeat customers for her mom, but she didn't say anything to dampen Daugherty's s excitement.

Daugherty took the boxes from Lizbet's grasp. "Now, I want you to go and sit with John and Gloria."

"I'd rather be helping you." Lizbet folded her arms and planted her feet.

Daugherty brushed a loose curl away from Lizbet's face. "We already had this conversation. Your grandmother will be here with Matias and Maria any minute to help."

"Elizabeth can't cart around trays and water pitchers," Lizbet said, returning to her favorite argument point.

"She'll be great," Daugherty countered as she turned away. She pulled open the refrigerator door and frowned at the platters of vegetables. "Do you really think anyone is going to eat these?"

"No." Lizbet boosted herself up onto the counter.

"Janet Peterson insisted on them." Daugherty turned

and caught sight of Lizbet parked on the counter. "What are you doing? You're not staying here."

"I'll feel awkward."

"I don't care. You should go for Declan."

"He won't even be able to see me. There's like a thousand people in the stadium."

"Then do it for me."

"You?"

"I need you to watch John and Gloria."

"Why? They don't even like each other."

Daugherty planted her hands on her hips and glared at Lizbet.

Lizbet sighed and slid off the counter. "This is dumb."

"Declan's your boyfriend."

"No one has ever said that," Lizbet muttered.

Daugherty arched an eyebrow. "No? What would you call him? The guy who spends every spare moment he can with you?"

"That's too long." Lizbet smirked. "I call him Declan, because that's his name."

Daugherty placed her hands on Lizbet's shoulders and steered her toward the door. "I love you, but I don't have time to argue with you. Please go and sit with your boyfriend's parents and be a part of his graduation ceremony."

"Are you sure?"

The door opened and Matias and Maria entered, each carrying a giant orange plastic water cooler. Elizabeth and a wagon filled with watermelons followed.

"I almost lost one of these puppies," Elizabeth said as she stopped the wagon in the center of the room. "It rolled across the parking lot and came within inches of Mark Platter's SUV's tires. Matias rescued it from a life of watermelon sludge. You should have seen him. He was a thing of beauty."

"He's always a thing of beauty," Daugherty said, smiling at him.

Matias flushed beneath her observation. His eyes slid to Lizbet's, checking to see if she'd noticed. Dressed in black pants and a white button-down shirt that offset his dark skin, hair, and eyes, he was—as her mom had said—a thing of beauty.

Maria, his sister, snorted. "You have obviously never seen him—or smelled him—after soccer practice. If you had, you would call him an odiferous troll."

"Trolls can be useful," Daugherty said. "They're strong—"

"Strong smelling," Maria interjected.

"We don't have time for sibling squabbling," Daugherty said. "We've got to get these melons sliced up." She passed out knives and cutting boards.

Lizbet held out her hand, but her mom just frowned at her. "Get!"

Matias and Maria both sent Lizbet questioning looks. Since Lizbet sometimes felt awkward with Matias, she gave up with a shrug. "I'll be back right after the ceremony

to help," she said over her shoulder.

She passed through the mostly deserted hallway, trying to imagine what it would have been like to have attended a public school. She'd been homeschooled, first taught by her mom on Blackstone Island, and then tutored by Maria and Matias when she'd come to stay with Elizabeth. She'd done well on her SATs and already signed up for courses at the Queen Anne Community College. The woman at the advisement center had told her that after she completed her associate degree, she'd be able to apply to any school she wished, and if she wanted to attend a Washington University they would accept her college credits.

But Lizbet's problem was she really didn't know where she wanted to go from there. She paused in front of the gym doors, admiring her mom's work. Daugherty had collaborated with the PTA board and mostly used the decorations from years past, but she could make even dog-eared streamers, flags, and garlands look good. She'd steered the committee away from the traditional balloons and used Dr. Seuss's book *Oh, the Places You'll Go* as the theme. She had asked students from the art department to paint posters mimicking Dr. Seuss and all the decorations matched his crazy color scheme.

Oh, the Places You'll Go. It seemed like a mockery to Lizbet. Declan would go to Duke. She'd be left behind.

The high school band began to play and Lizbet picked up her pace. She had a general idea of where to find the

football stadium and the music guided her. Outside, she spotted the crowd of seniors lined up behind the stands. She looked for Declan, but everyone looked so similar in their dark robes and funny square hats. Then she saw him in the white-robed crowd with a collection of ribbons and medals draped around his neck, standing next to Baxter who towered over everyone like a goose in a flock of baby chicks. Declan didn't see her. She didn't call out, but hurried through the gates, flashing her ticket at the kid standing sentinel. He pointed her toward the center section. John waved at her. Moments later, the band crashed into *Pomp and Circumstance* and Lizbet took her seat between John and Gloria. Despite the fact that she was surrounded by thousands of people, she'd never felt more alone.

Strange, when she'd lived on the island with just her mom and the animals for company she hadn't been lonely. It wasn't until she'd come to East End and her eyes had been opened to a vast world filled with people and complex relationships that she'd realized how different she was. She now knew that being alone didn't necessarily make you lonely. But being different definitely did.

There were about three hundred students in Declan's graduating class. Of course, not all of those were attending

grad night, but it seemed like it. The gym pulsed with music, laughter, and dozens of conversations. Game booths manned by teachers, parents, and volunteers lined the walls. Declan spotted the other guys from the basketball team shooting hoops through what looked like the Cat in the Hat's hat. He glanced around, hoping to catch sight of Lizbet.

She, along with her mom and the Hernandez twins, were catering and she had to be somewhere close. Knowing Lizbet, she'd probably spend the evening hiding in the kitchen. He smiled, trying to think of ways to draw her out.

He spotted Matias Hernandez refilling the water dispensers. His white button-down shirt offset his dark skin, hair, and eyes. His hair curled away from his forehead and his chin carried a hint of a beard shadow. Declan wasn't the only one watching Matias at the water coolers. Several girls gathered around him, cups held out, waiting for water and the chance to speak to him.

Matias laughed at something one of the girls said and filled her cup, but his laughter didn't touch his eyes. His attention moved behind the cluster of girls to the back of the room where Lizbet stood beside the cookie table, refilling the trays. Declan's stomach curled as he watched Matias watch Lizbet.

Like Matias, Lizbet wore simple black pants, a white button-down shirt, and a black tie. It was the most sedate thing he'd ever seen her wear. Her hair, normally so wild, had been pulled back into a tight bun at the crown of her head. He itched to set it free, and he wondered what she'd do if he did.

Someone elbowed him. "You're drooling, man," Baxter said. "Why don't you just go and talk to her."

Declan shook himself. "I can't. I promised her mom I wouldn't distract her. This job is really important to Daugherty and she wants everything to look professional. I offered to help, but..."

Declan glimpsed the ring-toss booth manned by his mom.

Baxter intercepted and interpreted the look. "Your mom doesn't approve?"

"It's not that she doesn't approve of Lizbet. She thinks it's silly to start a relationship when I'm leaving for Duke in two months."

"Hmmm," Baxter murmured in his annoying I-know-everything way.

"What does that mean?" Declan practically growled.

"Well, you know it's typical for females, especially mothers and their potential daughters-in-law, to engage in power struggles."

Declan pushed Baxter in the chest, but the mammoth didn't budge. "I'm not marrying Lizbet."

Baxter just raised an eyebrow.

"At least not anytime soon," Declan muttered.

"Doesn't matter. I'm sure your mom still sees her as a threat."

"To what?"

Baxter rolled his eyes. "For the last eighteen years, your mom has been the leading lady in your life. It's hard for any mother to relinquish that."

"My mom's not like that." Declan angled away from Gloria. He knew that she wouldn't be able to hear him over the noise, but he didn't want to take the chance. "She has enough of her own drama to worry about."

"Then why was she warning you off Lizbet?"

Declan rolled his eyes. "She wasn't... Not exactly."

Baxter pointed his cup at Lizbet and Matias. Lizbet held the cookie tray while Matias transferred the cookies to the platters on the table. They worked seamlessly together, almost as if their movements were choreographed. Declan knew they were tight friends.

When he left for Duke, Matias would still be around. He was going to the University of Washington on a soccer scholarship. Hopefully, he'd be so busy practicing breakaways he wouldn't have time to flirt with Lizbet.

Baxter grinned. "You got it bad..."

"Shut it." Declan threw his elbow into Baxter's gut before striding across the gym. Nicole intercepted him.

"Hey. Have you tried the whack-a-mole?" Light from the disco ball sparkled on her blond hair.

He didn't know how to tell her that at that moment the only thing he wanted to whack was the guy laughing with Lizbet. Both of Lizbet's hands were occupied with the cookie tray, so Matias held a glass of punch to Lizbet's lips for her to drink. The gesture, in Declan's mind, crossed the line between friendship and intimacy.

"Come on." Nicole took his arm and tugged him toward the whack-a-mole booth.

Declan felt his mom's attention following him as he allowed Nicole to tow him across the gym.

"See the giraffe?" Nicole pointed at the yellow and blue stuffed animal. "My baby brother loves giraffes and you only have to hit ten moles in two minutes to win one."

Declan knew Nicole's little brother had Down Syndrome.

"You'll get him one, right?" Nicole looked at him with her pale blue eyes.

Declan sought out Lizbet. The cookie platters had been restocked, and she and Matias had disappeared.

"Sure," Declan said, giving the attendant a ticket and picking up the giant rubber hammer. As he nailed the mechanical mole heads popping out of the circles of AstroTurf, he imagined that each of them was Matias.

John and Daugherty stood side by side, assembling sandwiches. They looked good together, like they belonged. Lizbet tried to imagine what would happen if they decided to marry. What would that mean? She would always be

connected to Declan and she wasn't sure how she'd feel about that. Of course, it would be great if they stayed together, but what if he went to Duke—as he assuredly would—and met and fell for a co-ed? Where would that leave her? She imagined sharing a string of holidays with her mom, John, and Declan and his wife and children, and her stomach rolled.

Daugherty glanced at Lizbet over her shoulder. "You okay, babe?"

Lizbet nodded. "I'm just... I don't know. I'm fine." She quickly loaded up another tray of cookies. Holding the platter above her head as she weaved through the mass of students, she made for the refreshment table. A siren sounded and lights began to flash, signaling that someone had won an arcade game. She looked up from her catering detail to see Nicole with a giant giraffe tucked under her arm, kissing Declan.

Lizbet's world shifted. Keeping her head down, she quickly transferred the cookies from the tray to the platters on the tables. Feeling sick, she bolted for the open door.

The night air tingled against her skin. Leaning against the brick building, she tipped her head back and stared at the stars dotting the dark sky. Their beauty couldn't compete with the memory of Declan and Nicole kissing.

Nicole was the sort of girl Declan belonged with. They were both going to Duke. They had grown up in the same sort of society. Lizbet understood that she didn't fit into their world.

But sometimes she felt as if she didn't belong in anyone's world.

"Here." Matias appeared at her elbow. He handed her another cup of punch.

She smiled at him, took the cup, and drank it all in one swallow. The cool liquid burned down her throat, making her gasp. "What was that?" She wiped her lips with the back of her hand.

"Punch?"

Lizbet shook her head. "It's not the same punch I had a moment ago."

Matias's eyebrows shot up. He took the cup from her, sniffed it, and softly swore. "Vodka?"

Lizbet shook her head. "I wouldn't know."

"I better go and tell your mom." But he didn't leave. "Are you going to be all right?"

Lizbet nodded. "I'm just..." She placed her hand on her belly, feeling sick. "Tell my mom I'll be right in."

Matias nodded.

An opossum lounging in a maple tree beside the science building bared his teeth at Lizbet. *"Are you ill?"*

"Maybe. I feel more stupid than anything." She closed her eyes and leaned back against the science building.

"Well, if it's smarts you're wanting, I suppose you're in the right place," the opossum said.

She peeked open an eye. The opossum twitched his tail at her. "So you think I should go to school, too?"

The opossum stared at her with his black beady eyes

but didn't reply.

"It's just so expensive. To me, it makes more sense to stay at the ranch with Elizabeth, help out with my mom's business, and work at the nursery."

"Is that what you want to do?"

She couldn't follow Declan to Duke and she'd never get in—at least not for a while. Maybe Declan wouldn't even be there by the time she finished her associate degree. "I can't do what I want to do," she said through clenched teeth. Right now, she wanted to punch Nicole and Declan in their bellies.

Declan pulled away from Nicole in time to see Lizbet dashing out through the wide double doors. As a student, he wasn't allowed to leave the building, whereas Lizbet could come and go as she pleased. He followed her anyway.

Nicole grabbed at his arm, but he shook her off. He passed the refreshment table where a group of teachers clustered around the punch bowl. Knowing he'd be caught if he used the same doors he'd seen Lizbet pass through, he slipped into the locker room and out the back door.

The dark night, so different from the commotion and noise in the gym, calmed Declan. So what if Lizbet had seen Nicole kiss him? She'd understand, wouldn't she? It hadn't meant anything. But a voice in the back of his head told him it would mean a great deal to Lizbet.

He found her outside the science building, pressed up against the wall, gazing at the tree. Something skittered in the branches above her head. She turned to him.

"Lizbet," he began.

She shook her head and held out one flexed hand, palm facing him like a traffic cop. "I can't talk to you right now."

He stepped closer and pointed at the gym. "Back there. It's not what you think."

"How do you know what I think?"

She looked unusually pale, and her eyes, typically warm, were cold and swimmy with tears.

His stomach clenched. "Lizbet," he began again.

"Don't," she said, right before she doubled over and vomited.

The bird who has eaten cannot fly
with the bird that is hungry.
— Omaha

Chapter Three

Declan froze. "You're sick."

She shook her head. "Vodka."

"Vodka?" Declan turned to Matias coming through the wide doors and his voice hardened. "You gave her vodka?"

"I didn't give her vodka... at least not intentionally."

"So you did give her vodka?"

Matias saw the vomit, and took Lizbet's elbow. He shot Declan a dirty look. "Come on," he said to Lizbet, his voice soft. "I'll take you home."

"I'll take her home," Declan said. He wanted to step closer, but the vomit separated them.

Matias's jaw hardened. "You've done enough already. Go back to the party."

"If anyone is taking Lizbet home, it's me," Declan insisted.

"Sorry, school boy, you're not allowed to leave." Matias curled his lips, and took a protective step in front of Lizbet.

Declan decided to ignore the vomit and lined the toes of his sneakers up against Matias's black boots. "You're not going to stop me."

Matias shoved Declan back a half step.

"Stop this," Lizbet said, looping her arm around Matias's. "Please."

Declan's breathing accelerated and he curled his hands into fists.

"Declan?" Gloria, followed by his dad, emerged from the wide double doors. "What's going on?"

"Son," his dad said, "you know you're not supposed to be out here."

Declan tipped his head at Matias. "He gave Lizbet vodka."

"No I didn't," Matias said, scoffing. "I wouldn't do that. Intentionally."

"That's a pretty serious accusation, son," Declan's dad said.

Declan bit his lip.

"Let's just all go and talk about this calmly and rationally," his dad said, taking Declan's arm in one hand and Matias's in the other.

"Why don't you come with me?" Gloria reached for Lizbet's hand. "John, can you explain things to Daugherty?

Tell her I'm taking Lizbet to my house. She can lie down there and Daugherty can pick her up in the morning after grad night ends."

"I'll take her home!" Declan tried to duck out of his dad's grip, but John tightened his hold on Declan's arm.

"She's going with me back to the ranch!" Matias said.

"No," John said. "Matias, Ms. Westmoor needs your help, especially since Lizbet's leaving. And you—" He shook Declan's shoulder. "You need to cool down. I'm not leaving you and Lizbet alone in a house overnight."

Declan tried to tamp down his rage. "What is that supposed to mean?"

"It means I'm not stupid," his dad said.

"You don't trust me?"

"You shouldn't trust yourself," his dad retorted.

"She's sick!" Declan twisted away and stormed back into the gym, humiliated.

Lizbet mutely followed Gloria to her large golden Mercedes and climbed in the passenger door. "If we called my grandmother, she could come and get me," Lizbet said after she and Gloria were both buckled in.

Gloria leveled a glance at her before starting the ignition. "Do you really think that's a good idea?"

Lizbet swallowed and shrank back against the seat.

"Probably not," she conceded. Elizabeth would be in bed by now. Of course she'd come if Lizbet asked her to, but Elizabeth wasn't a great driver even in the daylight when she was wide awake. "I hate putting you out."

"Nonsense. It's no problem. My father's house has lots of rooms. We can probably find you something clean to wear." Gloria wrinkled her nose and steered the car out of the parking lot and onto Sycamore Street. "Besides, this will give us a chance to chat about Declan."

Lizbet wished she could disappear. Chatting with Declan's mom was almost as bad as vomiting at Declan's feet.

"You know Declan is going away to school in the fall." This was not a question, but a statement.

"I know." Lizbet stared out the window at the dark trees flashing by.

"So, you understand this little fling will be short-lived." Gloria tightened her grip on the steering wheel.

"I would never ask Declan to change his plans for me," Lizbet said.

"Good." Gloria smiled, but it looked strained. "He's going to go to med school, like my dad."

"I thought your dad was a businessman."

"He was, but before that he practiced medicine, a surgeon. He had to stop when he developed arthritis."

"That's so sad," Lizbet said.

Gloria looked surprised. "Why, yes, I guess it was. He was always so successful, I never considered that he may

not have wanted to give up medicine." She threw Lizbet a glance. "What are your plans, dear?"

Lizbet bit her lip and then repeated what the academic counselor at the college had told her. It probably didn't answer Gloria's question, but as far as Lizbet was concerned, it told Gloria more than she had a right to ask.

Lizbet woke to find a black snout inches from her face.

"Oh good, you're awake," Rufus whined. The husky placed his nose on her arm and stared at her with his big blue eyes.

Lizbet thought about pointing out that her wakefulness was more about him than about her, but decided she needed at least one friend in the house. She scooched up onto her elbows and took in the room. According to Gloria, this had once been her Aunt Midge's room. It looked and smelled like it had last been decorated in the eighties. Even the sheets, which she'd helped Gloria put on the bed, smelled musty.

"Do you need to go out?" Lizbet asked Rufus.

He cocked his head, studying her. *"I'd rather talk. I'm glad we can talk. It's lonely here. I don't miss Godwin, because I hate him, but he used to take me on walks where we'd meet up with other dogs, squirrels, and the occasional cat. Not that I like cats any more than I like Godwin. It's really a toss-*

up which one I despise more. Cats, of course, are insolent, disrespectful creatures, largely selfish and arrogant… but then, of course, the same adjectives could be used to describe Godwin. But Godwin did walk me and would toss me a bone here and there, whereas a cat rarely provides any act of service to anyone other than itself."

Lizbet sat up, swung her legs to the side of the bed, and plucked at the white cotton nightgown—one of Aunt Midge's castoffs. Briefly, she wondered what had become of Aunt Midge, and why wasn't she inheriting the house? She glanced at the mantel clock on the dresser. 7:00 a.m. "Is Declan home?" she asked.

"That's who I need to talk to you about." Rufus jumped onto the bed and sat facing her, his expression earnest. *"I'm worried about him."*

Lizbet's mind wandered back to Declan and Nicole's kiss. She wasn't worried about him. She was more concerned about herself. She didn't want to get hurt and building her life around Declan seemed like the perfect way for that to happen.

"Why?" she asked.

"Godwin wants the Forsythe fortune, and if Gloria and Declan are both out of the way, he'll inherit."

The sleepiness Lizbet had been fighting suddenly fled. She thought back to her last encounter with Declan's stepfather. He'd been shooting a gun at their boat and both she and Declan had nearly drowned. Of course the man was dangerous. "But no one knows where he is."

"That's not true. I know where he is…or at least was."

"Where?"

"At his house."

"Gloria's house? How do you know that? Have you been there?"

He nodded his big furry head.

"You saw him there?"

"No, but I smelled him. And smell is more reliable than vision."

Lizbet knew that was true, especially for dogs. "But what can we do about it? The police are watching for him. Declan told me they have video cameras set up."

"I want to go. I need you to take me."

"What, now? It's at least three miles—six miles round trip."

Rufus blew out a juicy sigh and laid his head on his front paws. *"I need to go back, but they keep me locked up."*

She ruffled the fur between his ears. "It must be hard to be the dog."

A knock on the door silenced her.

Rufus whined and jumped off the bed.

"Come in," she said.

Declan came in, patted Rufus's head, and gave Lizbet an uncertain smile. "Hey, I'm glad you're here."

She lifted an eyebrow, waiting.

"About last night..." he began.

"Don't." Lizbet stopped him and ran her fingers through her curls, trying to tame them. She didn't want to know how mussed she must look. "You don't need my permission to kiss Nicole..."

"I don't want to kiss Nicole!"

"Last night you did."

"No, I didn't." He crossed the room in three long strides.

When he sat beside her, she inched away. "I know what I saw, Declan."

"You saw Nicole kissing me."

"You seemed like a happy and willing participant." She placed her hand on his leg and gave him a gentle squeeze. "And it's okay. In a few months you're going away to school. I'll stay here. For years. We can't... we shouldn't..."

"What are you saying?"

"We can't put our lives on hold."

The color drained from his face. He sucked on his lower lip as if to keep it from forming words he'd regret. "If I'd seen you kissing another guy, I wouldn't be all—all—" he stammered while he searched for the right thing to say.

"I'm just being honest."

"You're being cold. So cold." He looked at her as if he didn't recognize her.

"But realistic, right? You're going away. I'm staying here."

He stood and pushed his hand into his hair. "That's not happening today. We don't need to think about it now."

"But it's going to happen soon."

Rufus whined. *"Tell him to take me to Godwin's house."*

Lizbet shot the dog a quick glance. "The dog needs to go out."

"That's not what I said!" Rufus gave a quick bark.

Declan put his hands on his hips. "I'm not kissing anyone else but you." He waited, and she knew that he wanted her to tell him the same thing. And it wasn't that she particularly wanted to kiss anyone else, but she knew that once he was gone anything could happen.

"That's your decision."

"Wrong answer." Declan glowered at her.

Rufus barked. *"You have to warn him about Godwin!"*

She stood. Grabbing Declan's T-shirt, she pulled him so close she could feel his heat radiating through Aunt Midge's nightie. "I don't want to kiss anyone else but you, but—"

Declan kissed her hard. "No buts," he said after the kiss. He placed his forehead against hers and stared into her eyes. "The thought of you with someone else makes me nuts."

"You were the one kissing Nicole," she pointed out.

"No, I was the sack of stupidity being kissed by Nicole."

Lizbet ran her tongue over her furry teeth. If she had morning breath, Declan didn't seem to mind because he kissed her again. This time, she held onto his T-shirt because she was afraid if she didn't, she'd fall.

Declan took a quick shower while Lizbet slipped back into last night's clothes and pulled her hair into a ponytail.

Downstairs, she found Gloria in the kitchen pulling a carton of orange juice and a yogurt container from the fridge.

They exchanged greetings, and Lizbet put her hand to her lips, hoping that Declan's kiss hadn't left telltale signs.

Gloria sighed. "I'm not quite used to staying here. It's weird, you know? This was my childhood home. As a grown-up, I don't really feel like I belong." She opened and closed drawers, looking for utensils. She finally found a spoon and offered one and the yogurt to Lizbet before sitting down at the table. "If I'm going to live here, I need my own things. Right now, I feel as if I'm camping."

"Do you want Declan and me to help you move in?" Lizbet rested her hands on the back of a kitchen chair.

Rufus wiggled with excitement. *"Me, too. Take me!"* His words came out in three short barks.

Gloria frowned at him. "You just went outside!" She went to the door and flung it open.

The dog sat on his haunches and stared at her.

"Honestly! This dog!" Gloria settled back into her chair and peeled the lid off her yogurt.

"Is he yours or Godwin's? Because he seems really attached to you and Declan."

Gloria wrinkled her brow. "Well... Godwin bought him, but I guess he's always been more mine than his. Probably because I'm home more." She ran her hand absently over his head. "I'm glad he stuck around even though Godwin didn't."

Godwin belonged in an awkward conversation territory that Lizbet didn't want to enter. She cast about for something to say. "Declan and I could go to your house and pick up some of your things, if you'd like."

"Oh! I do need to do that. I can't just send the pair of you, even though I'd really like to."

"Send us where?" Declan entered the kitchen. His hair was still wet from the shower and his T-shirt stuck to his barely dry chest.

"The house. If this is going to be my new home, I need to make it so."

"What will you do with Godwin's house?"

"I can't do anything with it. Technically, it' not mine. He had it before we married." Gloria used her spoon to scrape out her yogurt container. "But I can get my things!"

"We'd be happy to help you," Lizbet said.

Rufus and Declan both gave her looks. One told her that he wanted to go, the other not so much.

Rufus bolted from the Mercedes as soon as Gloria opened the back passenger door.

Gloria slipped her keys into her purse and shook her head. "Crazy dog. Rufus!"

The dog charged into the woods like a man on a mission.

"He'll be back," Declan said, climbing from his truck. Lizbet followed.

Gloria frowned at the woods surrounding Godwin's house. The pines and firs stood tall and straight like silent custodians. The house had dark, lifeless windows. It looked closed and unwelcoming. Gloria and Declan climbed the stairs to the front porch. Lizbet followed. She spotted a robin sitting on a low-hanging branch of a dogwood tree. She wanted to ask him if Godwin, or anyone else, had been around in the last few weeks, but she couldn't very well do that in front of Declan and his mom.

She jerked a thumb at the woods. "Do you want me to try and find Rufus?"

Gloria gave her a thankful look. "That would be great. I should never have brought him. He'll just be in the way."

"You could lock him in a bedroom or the laundry room," Declan suggested.

"He'll hate that," Gloria muttered.

"It's better than his getting lost," Lizbet said, turning away.

"I'll go with you," Declan said.

"Hold up there, cowboy!" Gloria put her hand on his chest, stopping him. "You and I have things to do."

Lizbet didn't wait to listen to the rest of the argument. She crossed the wide lawn and followed the trail Rufus had taken into the woods. Under the trees' canopy, the air felt cool and smelled of spring and new life. Birds swooped from branch to branch and squirrels chattered greetings.

Lizbet glanced over her shoulder to make sure Declan and his mom were out of earshot before she asked, "Has anyone heard or seen Godwin?"

The squirrels all yammered at once.

"They say that Gloria and Declan are in danger," Rufus said as he stepped out from behind a boulder. *"Godwin wants the Forsythe inheritance."*

"But he's not here," Lizbet said.

Rufus lifted his snout in the air, sniffing. "He's somewhere close, I'm sure of it." He bolted deeper into the woods.

Lizbet sat down on a boulder, waiting. She couldn't return without Rufus, and yet, she didn't want to follow him through the thickets and fallen branches. She pulled her knees up to her chest as her mind drifted to the lonely months ahead when Declan would be away at school. She tried not to feel sorry for herself, tried to muster some excitement for her own future, but without Declan it looked bleak.

Sometime later, Rufus returned. Leaves and twigs clung to his fur and his pale eyes burned bright. *"There will be an accident!"*

"What?"

"On July fourth when Gloria and Declan go boating. There will be an accident," Rufus panted.

"What sort of accident?"

"He intends for both of them to die!"

"So I have to keep both of them from going on the boat?"

Rufus nodded.

"Who told you this?"

"The birds. They heard him. Godwin was here."

Birds... Lizbet knew that the birds were the least trustworthy in the animal kingdome. But still. She had to say or do something. With Rufus by her side, she strode back to the house, not exactly sure what she could say or do that would prevent Gloria and Declan from going boating.

"But I thought Godwin's yacht sank," Lizbet said.

"It did," Rufus replied, *"but Declan's grandfather's boat still floats."*

"But why would Gloria go out on her dad's boat?"

"Every year, Gloria watches the fireworks over Eleanor Bay. Godwin expects her to do the same this year."

Lizbet chewed on her lip. She felt pretty confident that she could prevent Declan from boating on Independence Day. Gloria was an entirely different story.

"I know, we'll go out on John's boat!"

"Gloria is not going to go for that," Rufus whined.

Lizbet brushed the leaves out of his fur as they walked. "I'll think of something," she said. "But first, I need to talk to these birds."

Rufus looked up at the branches. *"You heard her,"* he said to a crow.

The crow stamped his claw, cocked his head, and cawed. Within minutes, the sky darkened and a host of birds filled the air. They settled on branches, knocking twigs and dust into the air. The air shivered from the hundreds of beating wings.

Lizbet spotted the largest raven. She knew that ravens,

crows, and magpies all belonged to the same noisy, rambunctious family and that generally the largest held the greatest power. "You saw Godwin?"

"Why do you ask?" the raven replied.

"He threatened me and my friends. I'm afraid of what he'll do should we meet again. Please, if you know anything, tell me so I can keep my friends and family safe."

"We will tell you what we know. In fact, we will keep you abreast of his movements and plans, but first you must make a pact with us."

This surprised her. The creatures she knew were generally gossips and loved to spread blather for the simple pleasure of showing off and being know-it-alls. Crows and ravens were not only cunning, they were also a tightknit clan and could be powerful allies. Suspicion tingled down Lizbet's spine.

"Such as?"

"You must keep your communication with us secret."

That was easy. It was something she did anyway, although she wasn't exactly sure why. Something niggled in the back of her mind, a memory or a warning, but she'd kept her ability to talk to the animals to herself. Her mind drifted back to her younger self passing along a warning from a fox to her mom. *"Better tell your mom to make sure the henhouse is locked up tightly. The latch you have now is inadequate,"* the fox had told her. *"When I'm hungry, I can't help myself."*

Mom hadn't believed her, and the next morning when three of the chickens were missing, Lizbet had been blamed for not locking the gate. Ever since that day, she'd kept her communications with the animals a closely guarded secret.

"Of course," she said. "You have my word."

"Lizbet!" Declan ran into the woods, his eyes wide. "Oh good, you're okay and you found the dog." He put his hand on his chest, catching his breath. "I saw the circling birds. It was like a scene from a Hitchcock movie!"

Lizbet rose from her perch on the boulder and gave the raven a conspiratorial wink.

"We will share what we know when you are alone," the raven cawed.

Lizbet waved her hand and the birds rose in a flurry of wings.

"Whoa," Declan breathed. "What is happening? Freaky birds..."

Lizbet took his arm and led him down the path. "Did you know that crows and ravens have a very organized society? They're actually very social and caring creatures, and among the smartest animals on the planet." She said this more to the birds than for Declan. She wanted the crows to know how much she admired them and would appreciate their help. "Not only do they mate for life, they are probably more attentive parents than most humans."

"I didn't know you were so into birds," Declan said.

"Not just birds—most creatures." She bumped him with her hip. "Like you."

Declan turned to her, wrapped his arms around her, and kissed her long and slow.

They spent the day boxing up Gloria's favorite things. When Declan's arms, chest, and back complained from hauling one too many boxes, Gloria collapsed in a wingback chair near the fireplace. Her jeans and white T-shirt were covered with dirt smudges. She pulled off the bandana tying back her hair and used it to mop her face. "Should we pick up Chinese for dinner?"

Declan rolled his shoulders. "Sure."

"Where's Lizbet?" Gloria asked.

"I'll find her," Declan said.

He took the stairs two at a time and peeked in each room off the upstairs hall. He found her standing at the open window of a secondary bedroom. She turned when she saw him. An expression he couldn't read filled her eyes. Then her features softened, and the worried lines around her eyes disappeared as she smiled at him.

Outside, a bird left its perch on the branch of an apple tree.

"You ready to go?" Declan asked.

"Of course," Lizbet said. "Does your mom have everything she needs?"

"Maybe, maybe not, but it's not like she can't make a second trip," Declan said as they tromped down the stairs. "It seems like such a waste for this house to just sit empty."

"Oh, it won't be empty for long."

"What do you mean?"

Lizbet blinked, then laughed. "Well, you probably don't want to hear this, but animals and critters will take up residence if no one else will."

Gloria must have overheard them because she joined in. "That's a horrible thought. Let's make sure the windows are tightly closed and the doors locked."

Lizbet just smiled, as if she knew something Declan and his mom did not. His thoughts skittered back to the bird in the apple tree, and earlier, the circling crows in the woods. It was almost as if... what?

The frog does not drink up
the pond in which he lives.
— Sioux

Chapter Four

I have to keep Gloria and Declan from going out on Eleanor Bay!" Lizbet told Tennyson, her cat, that night as they curled together on her bed. "And it's easy enough to do once, but according to the birds, Godwin's placed something in the boat's engine."

Tennyson stretched and yawned. *"Can't you just remove the something?"*

"I don't know what belongs in an engine and what doesn't. Besides, what if it blew up when I was trying to disable it?"

"Sink it."

"I can't do that. Can I?" She tapped her lips, thinking. After a moment, she threw back her covers, climbed from the bed, and retrieved her laptop.

Tennyson meowed a complaint at all the shuffling about, but snuggled back into place as Lizbet settled the computer on her lap. "Mmm, so Eleanor Bay is really part of Back Bay."

"So?"

"I don't know. I'm thinking..." Lizbet flopped back against her pillows. She knew the name of the boat, *Gloria Hallelujah*, named after Declan's mom, and she'd seen its picture. If she could get into the marina, she was pretty sure she'd be able to find it. But then what?

She tried to sleep, but every time she closed her eyes she envisioned the Gloria Hallelujah exploding into orange and red flames. After what seemed like hours, she fell asleep. In her dreams, sea creatures darted around the mast of the sunken Gloria Hallelujah. A mermaid bid her to follow to still, dark waters where a lifeless Declan floated, his arms spread wide, his eyes open, his hair splayed like a Mohawk gone wild. Lizbet woke with a start and bolted from the bed, her heart pounding.

She had to do something. Lying in bed was no longer an option. Somehow, someway, she had to prevent Declan and his mom from ever getting on that boat. The floor beneath her feet felt like ice, but she didn't care. She pulled a pair of overalls and a flannel shirt from her dresser, shoved her feet into a pair of boots, and tugged a black hoodie over her head.

"Where are you going?" Tennyson peeked one sleepy eye open.

"To the docks."

"What are you going to do?" Tennyson now had both eyes open.

"I'm not sure." But maybe a salmon would help.

While the moon hung as high as it could go, Lizbet led Trotter out of the barn. She adjusted his saddle and stuffed the frozen salmon into the saddlebag. Of course, it didn't fit all the way so its head poked up, its mouth gaped open, and its beady black eye glared at her as if it knew her plans.

"You stink," the horse said.

"Here." Lizbet drew an apple out of her hoodie's pocket. "I have something for you."

Somewhat appeased and not quite as cranky about being woken for a midnight ride, Trotter munched on the apple while Lizbet put one foot in the stirrup and threw the other over Trotter's back. According to the GPS, they would be able to take trails most of the way to Eleanor Bay. They could bypass most city streets, but a few times they'd have to cross bridges and navigate neighborhoods. Hopefully, they'd do it all in the dark.

They hadn't gone far before Trotter lifted his muzzle. His nostrils flared and his trot slowed. Lizbet urged him forward, but he balked.

"What is it?"

"I'm not sure." Trotter sidestepped.

Lizbet patted his neck reassuringly. "Come on, the sooner we deliver the salmon, the sooner we can get home."

Trotter blew out a noisy breath, bucked up his courage, and pressed forward into the dark night.

Lizbet tried not to worry about wolves, but dark shadows flitting through the trees kept her tingly awake despite the hour.

The moon cast long beams of light across Back Bay. Boats of all shapes and sizes were moored along the docks. Most would be empty, but she couldn't count on all of them being unoccupied. She led Trotter to a lamppost and tied his reins around it.

"This shouldn't take long," she told the horse as she patted his neck. "We'll be safe in the barn soon."

The horse looked skeptical, but he didn't say anything.

Lizbet drew the salmon from the saddlebag. It had thawed slightly on the long trip and now felt slimy and cold. She held it in front of her like a platter. Other than her footsteps echoing on the boardwalk and water slapping the pilings, everything was quiet and still.

Maybe this wasn't such a good idea. Where were the sea lions?

The chain-link fence surrounding the marina was seven feet high. Lizbet tossed the fish over to the other side before scaling the fence. She landed beside the fish, scooped it up, and went in search of the *Gloria Hallelujah.*

Like all the other boats in the marina, it was covered by an enormous nylon netting. Moonlight sparkled on the gleaming white hull, and water sparkled on the clean teak deck. She felt slightly ill knowing she would do what had to be done. Leaving the fish on the boardwalk, she got to work.

"Whatcha doing?" A seal popped his black head out of the water.

Lizbet smiled as her apprehension slowly drained away. "Unwrapping this boat."

"What for?" the seal barked.

"Well, I thought maybe you and your friends would like someplace comfortable to hang." Lizbet untied the ropes securing the net before rolling it up.

"Maybe I don't want to share."

Lizbet finished pulling back the net and rolling it into ball. She straightened and met the seal's stare. "You don't have to share, but that is a really big fish for you to eat all by yourself." She picked up the salmon and waved it in the air. As she had expected, several seals and sea lions poked their heads out of the dark water. Lizbet grinned and tossed the fish onto the deck of the *Gloria Hallelujah*.

The animals, of course, would trash the boat, but she needed to not think of it like that. If the birds were right, she was actually saving the boat. The animals would be much kinder than a bomb. Maybe.

The seals and sea lions grunted, slapped their fins, and squealed as they attacked the salmon.

"So... um... do you think you guys could hang out here?"

No one looked at her.

"I can bring more fish... All I ask is that you stay on this boat. Deal?"

It wasn't a long-term solution, or even a reliable one. After all, Lizbet knew seals and sea lions were notoriously slippery. But she also knew that the animals would hang around at least until tomorrow. But just to be sure, she stripped down to her bra and panties and plunged into the water. The cold enveloped her. She rose sputtering. Then she grabbed the tow rope and started the long swim out of the marina.

Pulling a boat laden with sea animals was not easy. Not that she had thought it would be. "Don't let me drown, okay?"

One seal rose and clapped his fins, applauding her. That was all the encouragement she needed. The bay rippled as she moved through it. She didn't meet resistance until they left the cove. There, the tide roiled and the boat bucked against the waves. Lizbet tugged at the rope and fought the waves for as long as she could.

She heaved onto the deck. The cold air raised goose pimples on her skin. Her arms and legs felt like wet noodles. She scooched the animals with her foot so she could reach the captain's chair. She plopped behind the wheel and pointed it at the rocks jutting out of the water. Inhaling several long breaths, she tried to regain

her strength. She would need it for what was coming next. Leaning back, she studied the star-studded sky. Then, when she thought she could, she ran and jumped off the stern of the boat. Mustering her depleted strength, she gave the boat a push. As she'd hoped, the *Gloria Hallelujah* hit the rocks with a sickening splintering of wood.

Exhausted, Lizbet headed for shore. She slept on Trotter's back all the way home.

Lizbet woke the next morning to the sound of yipping. When she crawled out of bed, every muscle screamed in complaint. She hobbled to the window and pulled back the blinds. The bright sunlight startled her. Considering her night, it didn't surprise her that she'd slept in, but she wondered why neither Elizabeth nor Daugherty had woken her to help with the morning chores.

She saw Elizabeth standing in the vegetable garden, hoe in hand. Beside her, Daugherty wore a large straw hat that protected her skin and shielded her face from Lizbet's view. They were both shaking garden tools at something. Curious, Lizbet tried to open the window, but her arms had the strength of a newborn baby.

She threw on a pair of sweatpants and a T-shirt and pushed her feet into her slippers. Only the pile of smelly wet underclothes on her closet floor gave a hint of her crazy night. She stumbled down the stairs.

"Scat!"

"Go away!"

Her mom and grandmother's voices floated through the open window. Lizbet grabbed a bowl, a spoon, and a carton of oatmeal, but on her way to the fridge for the milk, she paused.

Rufus sat in the middle of the garden staring at the house, impervious to Daugherty or Elizabeth's attempts at shooing.

Lizbet abandoned her breakfast and went to rescue the dog. He bounced up off his haunches as soon as he spotted her on the back porch. Lizbet sank to the steps. She was pretty confident she'd successfully squelched Gloria's boating plans for the day, and she wondered if Rufus had come with an update or a thank you.

He brushed against her and she scratched him between the ears.

"Do you know this creature?" Elizabeth asked, still wielding her shovel.

"He's Declan's dog."

"John has a dog?" Daugherty asked, sounding slightly hurt.

"No. Technically, he's Declan's stepfather's dog, so he lives with Gloria." She smiled at Rufus as she petted his thick fur.

"Well what's he doing here?" Elizabeth asked.

"I'm not sure."

"It's a hefty walk all the way from Godwin's."

"Remember, Gloria is living at her dad's house in the University District now."

Elizabeth blew out a surprised whistle. "That's even farther!"

"He must have something important to tell me," Lizbet said.

Daugherty and Elizabeth both laughed because they thought she was joking.

"I'll call Declan and get Rufus some water." Lizbet stood and brushed her hands on her sweatpants.

Elizabeth studied the dog. "He must really love you to come all this way."

"He was probably looking for his old home and got lost," Daugherty suggested. "I heard moving can be really traumatic for animals."

"Is that it?" Lizbet asked the dog. "Are you traumatized?"

"I had to thank you," Rufus barked.

Lizbet shepherded the dog into the kitchen and filled a bowl with water for him. She glanced out the window. Her mom and grandmother had returned to tending the garden. "You came all this way just to thank me?"

"And to enlist your aid."

"Of course. You know I'd do anything for Declan."

Rufus sat down and scratched his nose with his paw. *"I'm sure Godwin has been in our new house. Today, his smell lingers everywhere and yet as far as I know he has never been there before."*

"The one in the University District?"

Rufus nodded.

"Could it be that his smell came with Gloria's things?"

Rufus wagged his head.

"Interesting. I'll call Declan. Maybe I can think of a way of asking to view the security cameras' footage."

She picked up the landline and dialed Declan. Even before Declan could say hello, Gloria could be heard in the background, shrieking.

"Hey," Declan said, sounding tired.

"Wow, your mom sounds upset," Lizbet said. "What's going on?"

"The boat had an accident. Somehow it came untied and floated out of the marina."

Lizbet tried to sound surprised. "What do you think happened? It's okay, though, right?"

"No, it's not okay. It exploded."

"Exploded? But that's not possible." Lizbet fell into a kitchen chair, dimly aware of Rufus's curious scrutiny.

"It's so weird. Someone drove it out of the marina and then blew it up."

"No. That's not what happened." She caught herself. "That couldn't have happened. It doesn't make any sense. What about the seals and sea lions?" A sick feeling washed over her. The thought of her oatmeal turned her stomach.

"The seals and sea lions?"

"Well, there's always sea creatures around... I just hoped no one was hurt." She paused. "Do you think maybe Godwin did this?"

"Probably. We're going to watch the security videos in a few minutes. Mom's meeting with her clients is, of course, cancelled."

"Hey, here's something weird."

"Something else?"

"Rufus is here."

"What?"

"Yeah, I woke up this morning and found him in the garden. My mom and Elizabeth were trying to run him off."

"What's he doing there?"

"I asked him, but he dodged the question."

"So strange." The laughter in his voice told her that he thought she was joking.

"If I could drive, I'd bring him to you. He's welcome to hang out here as long as you need him to." She glanced at her cat sitting in the windowsill and hissing at Rufus. "Although Tennyson is not a fan."

Lizbet sat with Declan and Gloria on the den's sofa watching the security cameras' footage on the TV screen and trying not to fall asleep. Her aching muscles complained no matter what position she assumed. When a shadow appeared on the screen, Gloria bounced to her feet and aimed the remote. The screenshot froze, catching Godwin in a half step.

"He came in during Declan's graduation!" Gloria huffed. "Of course he knew we'd be gone then!"

"That still doesn't explain how he got in," Declan said.

"Someone must have given him a key," Lizbet suggested.

"We don't know that," Gloria said.

"It looked like he had a key," Declan pointed out.

"He has his back to the camera. He could have pried the lock... somehow."

Declan rubbed his forehead and looked out the window at the moving shadows.

"Someone had to have seen something," Lizbet said, addressing the dog.

Rufus settled onto the floor at Lizbet's feet and placed his shaggy head on his paws. *"There was no one here but a mouse."*

"A mouse!" Lizbet gasped.

"Where?" Gloria shrieked.

Lizbet scrambled for an appropriate response. "I thought I saw one!"

"You did?" Declan questioned.

Lizbet looked at Rufus, but he rolled onto his back and wiggled like he was scratching an itch.

"Over there." Lizbet pointed at a dark corner behind a potted plant.

While Gloria shrank against the sofa, and Declan went

to investigate, Lizbet nudged Rufus with her foot. "Some mouser you are."

Rufus's whiny response sounded like an out-of-tune violin.

Declan dropped to his knees to inspect the space between the urn and the wall. The plant had dropped a number of leaves.

"Get up and find the mouse!" Lizbet demanded of the dog.

Rufus rolled up to his haunches and made the violin noise again.

Declan rocked back onto his heels and brushed the leaves off his pants. He froze. "Poop. Augh," he said. "There really is a mouse."

"I told you." Lizbet came to investigate. All the dead leaves made her wonder how long it'd been since the tree had been watered. "Where do you think he's living?"

Declan shook his head and climbed to his feet. "But we're getting distracted. We want to catch Godwin—not a mouse."

For apparently no reason, Rufus gave a short bark.

Lizbet frowned at the dog. "I could bring over Tennyson," she said slowly.

Rufus barked again.

"Your cat?" Declan asked.

She lifted a shoulder. "He's a good mouser."

"Forget about the mouse!" Declan ground out.

"I can't forget about the mouse," Gloria piped up from

her perch on the sofa. "I don't know if I'll be able to sleep tonight knowing there's a mouse in the house."

"Godwin breaking into the house while we're gone doesn't bother you, but a mouse does?" Declan asked.

"Let me bring over my cat," Lizbet said.

"Are you afraid of mice?" Declan asked.

"No, not at all," Lizbet said. "But I get how your mom feels."

"We need a locksmith, an exterminator…" Gloria ticked items off on her fingers.

"An exterminator?" Lizbet sounded squeamish. "We just need to catch it, not kill it."

"Well, then what are we going to do with it?" Gloria asked, horrified.

"Release it into the woods?" Lizbet suggested.

Gloria sucked in a deep breath. "It will just come right back and, for all we know, bring back a crew of its mice friends with it."

"I'll take him with me to the ranch. He can live in the barn. It's safe, warm, and there are a lot of other mice to keep him company."

Gloria studied Lizbet. "It's a mouse. It's not like we're looking for a retirement community for him."

"I'm sure he'd rather live there than be exterminated!"

Declan brushed his hands together. "I'm calling a locksmith."

Gloria lifted her chin. "I'm calling an exterminator!"

Rufus barked.

"I guess I'll take the dog outside." Lizbet patted her leg. "Come on, Rufus." She led him outside, but stayed close to the house. Declan and his mom's voices floated out the window.

"Your girlfriend..." Gloria began.

"She really likes animals," Declan cut her off. "That's not a bad thing."

"Any virtue taken too far will become a vice," Gloria said.

"As far as I know, she hasn't taken to raiding animal shelters or joined any animal activists."

"How can you eat a hamburger in front of her?"

Declan laughed. "I didn't criticize you for marrying Godwin."

"You're not going to marry her, are you?" Gloria's voice rose in panic.

"I'm not marrying anyone anytime soon."

"That's good. And for the record, you absolutely did criticize me for marrying Godwin."

"And was I right or was I right?"

Lizbet peeked in the window, hating herself for eavesdropping, but unable to pull herself away.

Gloria sniffed. "You were right... for once."

Declan put his arm around his mom's shoulders. "I wish, for your sake, that I'd been wrong. I didn't like him, but I had no idea he would turn out to be so..."

"Evil?"

"That's a harsh word."

"He tried to kill you!"

Declan shook his head. "No, I don't think so. If he had really wanted to kill me, he could have. I think he was trying to scare us off."

"But why?"

"I don't know." Declan kissed his mom's cheek. "If he turns up, we can ask him."

"Assuming, of course, that he's not taking potshots at us," Gloria said darkly.

The late spring sun shared the sky with a daytime moon. Rufus rooted around the foundation of the house, sticking his snout into the bushes and beating the shrubs with his tail.

"Smell anything?" Lizbet whispered.

'No,' Rufus woofed.

"He'd better show himself before the exterminator gets here," Lizbet said. "Did you hear that, mouse? Gloria's going to get an exterminator!"

Squee!

Rufus's ears perked up. He lunged into a rhododendron bush. Lizbet grabbed his collar and yanked him to the lawn. "Sit!"

The dog sat, quivering.

"Let me talk to him," Lizbet said. She headed toward the rhododendron and Rufus followed. She wheeled on him. "Stay!"

He slunk back to the grass and flopped down.

"Come here, mouse," Lizbet coaxed. "I won't let anyone hurt you."

Squee!

Lizbet dropped to her knees and peered into the flowers. A small brown mouse quivered against the brick wall, his whiskers twitching like a fluttering leaf. "Ah, there you are!"

"Can you really take me someplace safe to live?" the mouse squeaked.

Lizbet nodded. "You'll be happy there. I can't promise you anything if you stay here."

The mouse flicked his tail toward the house. *"That woman, will she really hire an exterminator?"*

"I'm afraid so." Lizbet edged closer. "You'll have to trust me. Hiding here won't be good enough. I don't think she'll stop until you're found."

The mouse trembled, shaking the rhododendrons. Lizbet held out her hand. The mouse inched forward.

Rufus barked and the mouse bolted up Lizbet's sleeve.

"Lizbet?" Declan asked.

She climbed to her feet, trying to ignore the mouse scampering up her arm.

"What are you doing?" Declan asked.

"I caught a mouse." Lizbet held her arm out in front of her like a battering ram. "He ran up my sleeve."

With his mouth ajar, Declan watched the mouse-sized lump move inside Lizbet's sweater. He shook himself.

"Why aren't you freaking out right now?"

"It's a mouse, not a barracuda."

"But, ick."

"What's going on?" Gloria stepped out onto the back porch.

"Lizbet caught the mouse," Declan told his mom. "It's in her sleeve."

Gloria's eyes widened, the blood drained from her face, and she fell back against the wall. "Ew!"

"I know!" Declan scratched his head. "It's obviously bothering us much more than her!"

"He can't hurt me!" Lizbet shook her arm until the mouse landed in her outstretched palm.

Gloria shrieked.

Even Declan took a step back. "Don't mice spread the plague?"

"That was rats, about six centuries ago."

"Rats, mice, same thing," Gloria said.

Lizbet stopped herself before she rolled her eyes. "Can you take me home?"

"Is the mouse going in my truck?" Declan asked.

"Yes," she said through clenched teeth.

"Let's just flush it down the toilet," Gloria suggested.

Lizbet curled her fingers around the quivering mouse and tucked him into her pocket. "That won't work. He'll just come back."

"Not if he drowns!" Gloria said.

"I can't believe you just said that." Lizbet, burning with righteous indignation, turned to Declan. "I'm walking home."

"Lizbet!" He came after her.

She shook his hand off her arm. "I need time alone," she said, without looking back at him.

She waited until they were out of the city to start grilling the mouse. "You better tell me what you know, or I'm leaving you in the cat sanctuary."

"Cat sanctuary? Where's that?"

Good question. Lizbet thought for a moment. "It's also called Pearl Lee's Fish House." It was one of her grandmother's favorite restaurants and every time they'd been there, she'd always seen half a dozen stray cats loitering in the alley, waiting for fish bones.

The mouse trembled. *"I don't know anything!"*

"Tell me about when Godwin came to visit."

The mouse remained silent.

Lizbet followed the sidewalk to a bridge over the Melba River. She drew the mouse out of her pocket and held him by the tail above the raging water below.

SQUEE! He wiggled like a fish on a line.

"Now do you remember Godwin?"

"I don't know which one is Godwin! All of you people look alike to me!"

Lizbet considered this and thought he might be telling her the truth. She had a hard time telling crows apart, but she knew the crows could easily distinguish human faces. Crows, though, were probably more intelligent than mice. Or, at least, this one.

"Godwin is a big man with black hair and a widow's peak."

"Widow's peak?" the mouse squeaked. *"What's that?"*

"It's... oh, never mind. Did you see a tall dark man at the house a couple of days ago? Or just any men..."

When the mouse didn't answer, she began to swing him over the rail.

"Yes!" Squee. *"There were two men."*

"Two? What did they look like?"

"One tall and dark, one blond."

"Interesting. What were they talking about?"

"The blond man wants to kill the woman and boy. The dark-haired man just wants them out of the way."

She tucked the mouse back into her pocket and resumed walking, although more slowly as she thought. "I thought Godwin was the bad guy. Now you're telling me there's someone worse?"

"I didn't say that," the mouse squeaked from her pocket.

"Of course you did."

"Don't put words in my maw."

Lizbet tried to tamp down her frustration. If she were honest with herself, she'd admit that her anger wasn't only with the mouse, but a portion also belonged to Declan, his egocentric mother, and the entire situation.

"*Why do you talk to animals?*" the mouse asked, surprising her.

"It's funny, I was just wondering the same thing." She thought for a moment, wishing she could remember the first time she'd held a conversation with an animal, but it was impossible. It was like trying to recall her first step or the appearance of her first baby tooth.

"*Do you know any other humans who can talk to animals?*" the mouse asked.

"No. Do you?"

"*No.*"

They walked in silence while Lizbet tried to round up her circling questions. "All the other animals can communicate with each other—dogs, cats, pigs. What I mean is, you all make different sounds and yet your communication is flawless. It's not like the goats speak goat and horses only speak horse, so why is it humans can only talk to humans?"

"*Except for you,*" the mouse pointed out.

Lizbet scrunched her forehead in thought. "Do you really think I'm the only one? I find that really hard to believe." She scratched her head. "There's this movie, *Dr. Doolittle*, it's about a veterinarian who talks to animals."

"*Are you a veter-whats-it too?*"

"No. I'd have to go to a lot of school for that."

"*So a veter-person does more than talk to animals?*"

"They take care of hurt or sick animals. I'm pretty sure most of them can't talk to animals... Well, they can and probably do, but they can't understand what the animals say back."

The mouse snorted. *"It's gotta be hard to help someone if you can't understand them."*

"True, but suffering does seem to be a universal language."

"You should be a veter-person."

"Like I said, it requires a lot of schooling."

"So?"

"I don't know..." The truth was, school scared her. She'd never actually gone to school before, while almost everyone else started as little kids. The thought of signing up for eight years of schooling to become a veterinarian terrified her. She didn't know if she could pass a simple math class, let alone advanced chemistry or biology. Even though being a veterinarian did seem like a natural fit for her.

"Do you think being able to talk to animals is hereditary?" the mouse asked.

"No. My mom and grandmother both like animals, but they can't talk with them." She stopped herself. "But my mom isn't my biological mother. I keep forgetting... my real mother died when I was young. I can barely remember her. It is possible, I suppose."

"How about your dad, then?"

Lizbet shook her head. If her father was Godwin, as she suspected, then she knew he was such an awful person, he'd never be able to talk to animals. He wouldn't

have the empathy. Suddenly, the need to know about her family—her family of origin—tickled the back of her mind like an out-of-reach itch. She had to learn all she could about her mother, Rose. She had to know if Godwin was really her father, or just an abusive bully Rose had become involved with. She longed to know where Rose was from, who her ancestors were, and just anything she could find.

"Where are we?" The mouse peeked his head out of Lizbet's pocket when she stopped to open the gate leading to the front walkway.

"This is Godwin's house. You'll be safe here. The house is empty."

The colonial cast long shadows over the grass. The windows were dark and empty. She wondered if Godwin was there. It looked deserted, but looks, she knew, could be deceiving.

Squee! *"I thought I was going to a ranch with a barn occupied by a host of other mice!"*

Lizbet followed the brick path around the back, passing a sadly neglected rose hedge. The lawn also needed attention. Who would care for the house and yard now that Gloria had moved out and Godwin was on the run? "I need someone to tell me if they see Godwin! If he went to the Forsythe's house, I'm sure he'll try to come back here, too. And if he does, I need you to keep watch and tell me what you learn."

"Why should I?"

"Because if you do, you can come and live in my grandmother's barn."

"I want cheese."

"Cheese? Really?"

"And not just any cheese. Good cheese! Like Gouda or Munster."

"I'll see what I can do," Lizbet muttered.

"When can I expect it?"

They arranged that Lizbet would come by every day either before or after work, then she set him down on the back porch. "Are you sure you'll be able to find your way inside?"

"Easy peasy," the mouse said as he scampered off.

Everything the power does,
it does in a circle.

Chapter Five

Declan parked his truck in Elizabeth's driveway right beside his dad's truck. Awkward. It flashed through his mind that his dad might harbor similar feelings for Daugherty as Declan had for Lizbet. So weird. Of course, Daugherty wasn't Lizbet's biological mother, but still... He really hated thinking of either of his parents as anything other than his parents. He tried to shut down any speculation on his mom or dad's sex life. Sure, maybe they had to take care of their bio needs, but... ew.

This was sort of like him and his dad dating best friends, but worse, because Lizbet and her mom were closer than any best friends he knew of. And the thought of the two of them ever comparing notes on how he or his dad kissed sent his creep-o-meter skyrocketing. Declan leaned his forehead on the steering wheel and tried not to wonder what his dad was doing. Obviously, he was there to see Daugherty.

Declan liked Daugherty. Of course, the whole isolate-yourself-on-a-deserted-island-for-twenty-years thing was super strange, but he couldn't really blame her since she'd had amnesia. Or had she? What if Rose, Lizbet's real mother, had been giving Daugherty ginger root tea? It was possible, right? No one really knew what this Rose person was like. Or even who she was.

Declan sat up and braced his shoulders. He'd come to talk to Lizbet. He hated how they'd ended their last conversation. When he felt at odds with Lizbet, he felt at odds with the world in general. She had looked so disappointed in him, and he wasn't even a hundred percent certain why. The mouse. She couldn't kill the mouse. She would rather carry it in her pocket for three miles and find it a good home.

Admirable, but... crazy, too.

And she'd seen him kissing Nicole—or more accurately, Nicole kissing him. He was turning into a seething mess of disappointment, and he hated feeling like he'd let Lizbet down... again. And again.

He had to talk to her. When there was a wrinkle in their relationship, his whole universe was full of ruts and

potholes. Leaning back, he closed his eyes. But he didn't want to try to talk to Lizbet while his dad was hanging around. Because when he said he wanted to talk, what he meant was he wanted to kiss. He preferred kissing to talking and if Lizbet would kiss him, that would mean she'd forgiven him. And he didn't want to kiss Lizbet in front of his dad.

A voice.

He looked out the window. Lizbet stood by the split-rail fence chatting with a horse. The Arabian shook his head as if he understood everything Lizbet was telling him.

Wanting to hear the one-sided conversation without interrupting it, Declan quietly slipped from the truck.

The horse spotted him, whinnied, and shook his mane at Declan. Lizbet looked over her shoulder. Something flashed over her expression, but it was so fleeting, he couldn't catch it. Frustration? Disappointment? Anger?

He shoved his hands into his pockets and looked at the ground as he walked. The gravel scrunched beneath his feet. "Hey," he said, looking up at her, trying to read her reaction.

She touched his arm. "I'm sorry I walked out on you like that. Your mom..."

"She wanted to kill the mouse."

Lizbet nodded.

"I love that you're such a softie."

She studied him. "You don't think I'm weird?"

"Oh yeah." He grinned.

Pain flickered across her face.

"That's a good thing," he assured her. "You are... unique. Like a snowflake."

"I'm like frozen water?"

He nodded. "But not as icy."

Her lips twitched. "You suck at apologies."

He gave his dad's truck a quick glance before he wrapped his arms around Lizbet. She felt so good against him. She fit perfectly, like the last puzzle piece. "Want to go for a walk? Or have you had enough walking today?"

"It was a long walk." She pulled away from him and considered this. "I still want to show you that circle of stones I found."

He draped his arm over her shoulder. Together they headed for the path that led through the woods. The Arabian nickered and flicked his tail as they walked past.

A chill passed over Declan as a thought struck him. "Is the mouse still in your pocket?"

"No."

"Where did you put him?"

She waved her left hand at some nebulous far-off point. "Does it matter?"

"As long as it's not near my mom."

"It's not."

"Do you really have a problem with exterminators?"

She blew out a breath and her shoulders tensed. "The Bible says not to kill."

"Ever?" He slid a glance at her face. "That's not exactly true, you know. The Israelites were pretty much killing machines and those priests were sacrificing goats and sheep fairly regularly."

When she didn't reply, he added in a soft voice, "I'm sorry if I sounded irreverent."

She twisted her lips as she thought of an answer. Finally, she said, "I know you don't believe in the Bible."

"I probably should have used a different analogy."

"No... it was a good comparison. I guess."

"But?"

"I don't believe in killing animals just because."

"And I don't believe in cohabiting with them."

She turned and jabbed him in the chest with her pointer finger. "That's so not true. What about Rufus?"

"Rufus doesn't want to live with mice either."

"Have you ever asked him?"

He laughed softly, but sobered when she frowned. "You're serious."

She blew out a sigh.

"I'm really tired of disappointing you."

She folded her arms. "You're not disappointing me."

"I'm not?" He waved at her folded arms and stiff body language. "Because everything about you says you're angry with me and I'm not really sure why."

She laid her hand on his chest. It felt warm and he wondered if she could feel his heart beating. His pulse accelerated.

"I don't want to be angry with you," she said.

"Then stop."

"Okay, but you just can't kill animals because they're inconvenient or in your way."

"I haven't killed anything today."

"Oh, not today... well, so glad you're restraining yourself." She pushed her hands through her curls. "I guess I want to go back to the house."

"Lizbet..." They studied each other. "I'm not a mass murderer."

"I know," she said softly. "You're a good person. It's just... we're so different."

He thought about pointing out that she was the different one, not him. She'd been the one living alone on an island with no one but her mom, some books, and the animals to keep her company... Suddenly, everything clicked. "Oh geez, I'm sorry."

"For what?"

He gathered her in his arms. He thought maybe she'd resist, but she didn't pull away. She still fit. "I think I get it now. Growing up, the animals were your only friends."

"That's true," she murmured against his shirt.

"Let's not fight." His lips found hers. She fit and she tasted good. Like her mom's blackberry wine.

"I didn't know we were," she said after a long time.

"We weren't. But let's stop thinking about all the ways we don't belong and focus on how right we are together."

He kissed her again. "Like this... This is how we fit together."

That night, Lizbet dreamt of an Indian camp high on the top of a hill. An eagle with tawny feathers flew before her, guiding her through the copse of birches and meadows full of ferns. Boulders, tall and craggy, rose from the underbrush like soldiers lining the path. An earthy smoke hung in the air, its scent teasing her with a memory of another place and time.

The teepee's angular poles pointed at the sky in different directions. Music floated through the trees: drums, flute, a lone man half-singing, half-chanting. Lizbet's pace quickened, although she didn't know why. Briars and prickly sticker bushes pulled on her skirt and sweater, as if trying to prevent her return.

How could she return to a place she'd never been before? This she would have remembered. But there was so much hanging just out of her recollection. At the edge of her fingertips—a thousand memories that may or may not have belonged to her.

A woman dressed in a long brown dress with a rope-tied apron stepped in front of Lizbet, blocking her view of the men, women, and children dancing around a fire. The flames cast embers into the twilight sky. The sparks glowed as they arched above the dancers.

"Welcome, child," the woman said in a language that wasn't English but Lizbet immediately recognized. "We have been waiting this long time."

Lizbet wanted to reply, but she realized that although she could perfectly understand this woman with the long gray braids and keen green eyes, she didn't know how to form the words in reply. She resorted to English. "Where am I?"

"You are home."

The smoke made her dizzy. She knew, but she did not know, this woman. "Who are you?"

"I am Alo, but you will call me Mawmaw." She beckoned for Lizbet to follow. "Come."

Lizbet cast a long glance at the dancers, wondering how they would respond if she joined them.

"We have been waiting this long time," the woman said again, hurrying Lizbet along the trail.

"Where are we going?"

Away from the fire, the smoke cleared and Lizbet breathed easier.

"To the circle of stones," the woman replied without looking back.

"I've been looking for that," Lizbet said, forgetting about the dancers. "I found it once before, but since then, every time I returned I wasn't able to find it. I thought I'd be able to see it on an Internet map site because it's so large, and I know it's somewhere on my grandmother's property, so I have a fairly good idea where to look."

Lizbet swallowed, aware that she'd been babbling. The old woman hadn't once looked at her since they'd started down the path through the woods.

The trees closed in on them, blocking out the daylight. Or had night fallen? An owl swooped out of a cedar tree, his wings sending reverberations through the air.

"Are we almost there?" Lizbet asked. "I need to get back soon." Although for what, she didn't know. Her mom and grandmother would worry. Or would they? After all, this was a dream and she was asleep.

Until she wasn't.

Lizbet bolted upright. She took note of the moon hanging low on the horizon. Not yet morning. Tennyson softly snored on his corner of the bed. Lizbet lay back against the pillows, her heart slowing.

Could her mother have been Native American? Lizbet had green eyes, but so had that woman who had clearly been a Native American. Lizbet tried to recall the local Indian tribes and reservations. She had seen the exit signs along the freeway, but she'd never really given them much thought. She ran her fingers over her arms, trying to warm them as a chill shook through her.

The woman said she'd been waiting, but for what? And why? How was she connected to Lizbet? With questions weighing down her mind and chasing away sleep, Lizbet slipped out of the covers and padded over to her desk. She watched the fat, round moon hover in the sky while she waited for the computer to boot on.

She typed in "local Indian reservations" and was confronted with dozens. Resting her chin on her hands, she considered the screen. Then an idea struck her. She typed in "Pacific Northwest Native Americans with green eyes."

The next morning, after her chores, Lizbet headed into the woods, once again in search of the circle of stones. She wandered through the copse of birches, the fern-filled meadow, and past the tall and craggy boulders, but she couldn't find the Indian village or the circle of stones. She paused when she heard the roar of an engine.

A motorcycle zoomed toward her. Grinning, a man in dark leathers pulled up beside her. He pulled off his helmet. Matias.

"Hey there," he said. "What are you doing out here by yourself?"

She told him about her dream.

"And you actually thought you'd find it? Don't you know dreams take place in La La Land?"

"Not always." She kicked at a rock near her foot, feeling foolish.

"Well, whatever it is you're looking for, we can find it a whole lot faster on my bike. Hop on."

"Aren't you going somewhere?"

"Yeah. To an Indian village and a stone circle."

"It's a circle of stones, not a stone circle."

"What's the difference?"

"One is like a small Stonehenge. The other sounds like a petrified donut."

"Petrified donuts? I know how to find those. There are plenty at *mi abuela's*."

Lizbet hung back. The bike was big and noisy and she'd have to hold on to Matias to keep from falling off.

His grin widened. "Are you scared?"

"A little," she admitted.

"It's fun. I can even teach you how to drive."

"Really? Will I need a license?" She'd wanted to get one, but if she waited six months until she was eighteen she wouldn't have to take, and pay for, the driver's ed course.

"Not if you stick to the woods and trails. A cop won't chase you down in here."

Lizbet returned his smile. "So would you teach me how to drive this?"

"Probably not this one. It's a temperamental beast, but I have a smaller, tamer one that my dad taught me on. In fact, I'd give it to you, if you like."

She blinked. "Really?" A bike would be so much better for getting around on than Trotter, although she'd never tell the horse that.

"Sure. My ma is constantly nagging at my dad to clean out the garage. It would need some work. New tires, an oil change, maybe a new battery, but I bet we could get it up and running." He gave her a slow smile. "It would be fun. But climb on, see if you like it first." He placed his helmet on her head. It was warm, heavy, and smelled of his shampoo and sweat. Taking the straps, he tightened them under her chin, then waggled the helmet side to side to make sure it was secure. "Don't want you losing your head," he said before he threw a leg over the seat and straddled the bike.

She settled behind him, her thighs touching his, her hands on his waist.

He gave her a smile over his shoulder. "Where to?"

"Up the hill. The circle of stones is at the top." She didn't tell him that she'd tried unsuccessfully to find it before with Declan. Sometimes she wondered if it had also only existed in a dream.

Matias gunned the engine, startling Lizbet with the burst of speed. She wrapped her arms around his waist and held on as the bike hurtled up the hill, spewing dirt and twigs behind them. They bounced over rocks and through potholes while Lizbet peeked over Matias's shoulder. Birds fluttered past. Chipmunks chattered from the trees. Rabbits skittered through the ferns. A squirrel stood on the side of the path, calling out a warning. Lizbet ignored them all and held on.

The trees grew increasingly sparse as they approached the top. Large stones circled the clearing. One large altar-like stone with a slab of granite stood in the center.

She glanced overhead, hoping and expecting to see birds or squirrels, or anyone or anything, but the air was heavy with silence.

A thought or distant memory came back to her. *Draw not nigh hither: put off thy shoes from thy feet, for the place whereon thou standest is holy ground.*

Ask questions from your heart
and you will be answered
from the heart.
— Omaha

Chapter Six

"Leo suggested you accompany me to the Igasho Winery," Declan's mom told him when she rang the next morning.

"Why?" Declan scratched his head, thinking of all the things he'd rather be doing. Even though he couldn't see her and her tone had been level, Declan knew she was frustrated with him.

"Someday this business will be yours."

"What if I don't want it?" Right now, all he wanted was a shower and a bowl of Captain Crunchies.

"Then you'll have to hire someone to run it for you, but you'll still have to keep your eye on it. You don't want anyone cheating you."

He almost asked why not, but decided to let it go. It was too early to goad his mom. Still, she was undeniably more interested in the Forsythe business dealings, shareholdings, and investments than he was. He peeked at the alarm clock beside his bed. "What time are you going? I promised Mr. Neal I'd be in by ten."

"Why are you still working there? I told you, we're rich now. You don't need to keep watering and fertilizing the plants."

Declan swallowed. He liked earning his own money. Money that came from his mom always had strings attached and he didn't want to get tangled up in them. "What time are you going?" he asked again.

"Well, I wanted to go first thing this morning," Gloria huffed. "But if you have to be at the nursery..."

"Can we go in the afternoon?"

"I guess. I'm staging a house on Wishful Lane. I suppose I can do it before rather than after."

"We're rich now," he mimicked her. "You don't need to keep watering and fertilizing homebuyers."

His mom's voice turned hard. "I'm not fertilizing anyone. I made a commitment to the Schneider's and I'm going to honor it." She paused before adding in a small, almost sad voice, "I won't be selling real estate forever."

Declan swung his feet over the side of the bed. "Mom, you don't have to give up your job. If you like it—"

She cut him off. "We're talking about you, not me. What time do you get off work?"

He told her.

"I'll pick you up at your dad's house. Don't wear your work clothes. You need to act the part."

Of what?

"What is this place?" Matias rubbed his temples and blinked slowly.

"Are you okay?" Lizbet asked, putting her hand on his arm and wondering if he felt the same as she did.

He shook his head and sat down on a nearby boulder. "Sorry. I..." He pulled off his shoes and socks and flexed his toes.

"Why are you doing that?" Lizbet asked, wanting to know if he'd had the same impression.

"Doing what?" He stared at her as if he'd forgotten she was there.

"Why did you take off your shoes?"

He contemplated the sock in his hand. "I'm not sure," he said slowly.

Lizbet sat down beside him and removed her own sandals. She placed them on the boulder then walked to the center of the stones.

"Lizbet! Stop!" Matias stood, his face drawn and his expression worried.

"Why?"

"I don't... I don't know. Let's go." He looked around, searching the nearby woods. "This place is giving me the creeps."

"But why?"

He shrugged. "We don't have to know the reason for everything."

Lizbet returned to the boulder and sat to refasten her sandals. Matias stood guard, keeping watch on the trees as if waiting for something to jump out at them.

"You know, I've been here once before, and then I've tried to find it again and failed."

"Maybe it's magic. Maybe you have to be wearing blue to see it, or maybe it's only visible on the third Tuesday of the third month." He paused, then added, "I'm only half-joking."

"This is the sixth month."

"You know what I mean."

"We are near the solstice."

"I thought that was in winter."

"There's a summer one, too."

Matias shook his head. "This is crazy talk. Let's go. This place is sucking our brains and turning us into lunatics. Again, only half-joking." He took her hand and pulled her to the motorcycle.

Was he holding her hand because he liked her, or because he wanted to hurry her away? Or both? Was it wrong to hold hands with Matias and kiss Declan? How would she feel if she saw Declan holding hands with Nicole? Was it different from seeing him kiss her? Hurt flashed through her as the memory of Declan and Nicole returned.

Declan had to bend to kiss Lizbet, but Nicole was close to his height. Nicole could plant a surprise kiss on him—something Lizbet couldn't do without his cooperation.

Matias dropped her hand when they reached his bike, retrieved the helmet and placed it on her head. She smoothed her curls back and her hand brushed against his as he adjusted her straps. She took two steps back, feeling uncomfortable and apprehensive about straddling the bike and holding onto Matias. She thought about making an excuse and walking, but another thought—a more pressing one—hit her.

"In my dream, the Indian village was nearby. Let's look for it."

Matias balanced the bike against his thigh while he zipped up his leather jacket. "You know I'm half Native American, right?"

She nodded.

"And you also know that Indian villages with teepees and people dancing and chanting around fires went the way of the dinosaurs."

"Who said anything about people dancing or chanting?"

Matias flushed and grabbed the bike by the handlebars. "Get on," he growled. "We can look, but we aren't going to find an Indian village."

"I didn't mean to offend you."

"I know." He slung a leg over the bike and waited for her to climb on behind him.

"You're lucky that you know your ancestry. I don't have a clue about mine." She settled behind him and placed her hands on his waist.

"If you had brown eyes, you could be Native American," Matias said before he started the bike.

"Maybe there are green-eyed tribes." She had to yell to be heard over the engine's roar.

"I've heard of green-eyed monsters, but not green-eyed Native Americans," he said over his shoulder before gunning the engine and sending the bike skittering down the hill.

Lizbet pressed herself against him and held on as they raced through the woods. Moments later, they came to a clearing and concrete parking lot surrounding a large building.

"Where are we?" she asked in his ear.

"A modern-day Indian village," he said.

He drove through the crowded parking lot to the front of the Kenda Casino. He slowed as they approached the entrance. "Want to go inside? It's not just about gambling. They have some artifacts and information on the Magena tribe."

"Do you mind?"

He shrugged. "I don't have anything going on today. How about you?"

Lizbet knew what he was really asking: where was Declan? She ignored the hidden question. "I would love to learn about the Magena Indians." The woman in her dream had green eyes and while she knew that dreams were usually grounded in fantasy more than fact, she couldn't help wondering if her mother had been a Native American.

Matias pulled into a parking space and cut the engine.

Although many of the employees looked Native American, most of the clientele appeared to be retired senior citizens eager to try out the buffet and lose their money on the slot machines.

"In a few weeks at the peak of the summer, people will come here by the busload," Matias said as he guided her through the wide glass doors. Inside, the floor was a stunning mosaic of gold and beige tiles with a salmon motif. A giant bronze statue of flying fish rose from a water-spewing fountain. Dark wooden beams crisscrossed the soaring ceiling. Beyond the foyer came the mingled sounds of jingling slot machines, and laughter.

Matias placed his hand on the small of Lizbet's back and guided her to a set of glass-encased shelves housing pottery, arrowheads, intricately carved pipes, and yellowing maps.

"These are all from the Magena tribe?" Lizbet asked.

Matias nodded. "My grandfather and uncles still attend the tribal council meetings. They have invited me to come, but my father forbids it."

"Why?" Lizbet tore her attention from the artifacts to glance at Matias.

He kept his focus on his hands. "He wants us to assimilate. He regrets not learning English and pursuing an education. He wants Maria and me to be true Americans." He made air quotes around the last two words.

"Learning about your mother's culture doesn't stop you from being an American! In fact, you could argue being a Magena is more American than—"

"I know, but I have to respect my father's wishes, even if I don't completely agree with him." He looked up, hopeful. "Would you like to meet my grandparents? They live on the reservation. They could answer your questions better than anything we can find here."

When she nodded, he took her hand and guided her back outside to the motorcycle.

"According to my father, the Kenda casino brings in millions of dollars a day," Matias said over his shoulder as they sped out of the parking lot and headed toward the Puget Sound. "But, as you can see, very little of the money actually falls into the hands of the people."

The twisting road through the tall pines led past weed-infested yards filled with rusting cars and lopsided trailers. Dogs of all sizes and breeds ran after the bike.

"My grandparents both have an alcohol problem, as do my uncles. But it's early in the day. We should be okay." Matias had to yell over the engine's roar and the dogs' barking. The wind snatched his words away.

"Will they mind our dropping by?" She spoke directly in his ear.

"No, my grandparents love company. They resent how little they see of my mom, Maria, and me. They blame my dad, of course, because it is his fault. He has done his best to shun his own culture, and he cannot understand my mom's desire to stay connected to her people."

The trees gave way as they approached a cliff bordering the Puget Sound. The early afternoon sun sparkled on the water and a few clouds wisped across the sky. As Matias turned off the main road and followed a dirt road down the bank, the bike's tires spewed mud behind them. He stopped in front of a moss-colored wood-frame house. An aged dog, part hound and part something else, rose from the mat on the front porch and came to greet them on shaky arthritic legs.

Matias climbed off the bike, held it for Lizbet as she did the same, and popped the kickstand. "This is Kudo," he said, fondling the dog's ears.

"How do you do, Kudo?" Lizbet greeted the dog.

He woofed, cocked his head, and watched her with swimmy eyes dim with cataracts. *"I haven't seen your kind in a moon's age."*

Surprised, Lizbet dropped to her knees so she could be nose to snout with the dog. "What do you mean?"

"What does Kudo mean?" Matias asked. "Do all names have meanings?"

"Your breed hasn't passed this way in a long time."

"Breed?" Lizbet muttered.

"Who knows?" Matias knocked on her helmet, reminding her to take it off.

Lizbet climbed to her feet, waiting for Kudo to answer her. She pulled off the helmet and handed it to Matias.

He draped the helmet's straps over the bike's handlebars.

Lizbet petted Kudo's giant head, silently willing him to tell her more.

"Green-eyed Magena-girl," Kudo whined. *"You are indeed rare, not only in appearance but in abilities."*

"But you've known others?" Lizbet asked.

"Like Kudo?" Matias ruffled the dog's ears. "Nah. Good thing, too. He's an ugly mutt."

Kudo blew out a derision.

"Ah, he didn't mean it," Lizbet consoled the dog. "You're a fine creature."

The door banged open and a small wizened woman emerged from the house. She wore a large flannel shirt, a baggy pair of jeans, and a bandana wrapped around her gray-streaked dark hair. "Matias!" She held out her arms.

Matias stooped to give his grandmother a kiss. "Mawmaw," he said, straightening. "I want you to meet my friend, Lizbet. She has some questions about our people."

Even though Matias's tiny Mawmaw had intelligent eyes and vibrant energy, Lizbet wondered if Kudo would have more answers for her. "I know so little of my real mother. I thought she might be Magena."

Mawmaw stepped off the porch, drew closer, and laid a withered palm on Lizbet's cheek. "Perhaps."

Matias raised one eyebrow. "You've seen green-eyed Magena?"

"It's not impossible. In fact, there is a legend of the Ollos Verdes folk. They say that the Ollos Verdes can talk to all nature."

"Nature, like animals?" Lizbet's voice squeaked.

"Not just animals," Mawmaw said. "But all nature— plants, weather, the moon and stars."

Lizbet touched her forehead and wavered on her feet as a dizzying wave washed through her.

"Are you unwell, child?" Mawmaw asked.

"Yes, but I want..." Lizbet stumbled over her words and her feet.

Matias grabbed her elbow and steadied her.

Lizbet pulled upright. "I want to hear more about the Ollos Verdes."

"Then come sit down." Mawmaw motioned to a pair of rocking chairs on the porch. "'Tis a story best told with a glass of wine."

"Mawmaw." Matias used a warning voice.

"It's just blackberry juice," Mawmaw persisted. "It can harm no one." She waved at the chairs. "Sit!" She pulled open the door and disappeared into the house.

Matias rolled his eyes and pulled the wooden rockers side by side. Lizbet sank into one as Matias settled into the other.

Mawmaw, with a bottle tucked under her arm and three glasses in her hands, pushed through the door. She placed the glasses on the porch railing, uncorked the bottle, and filled the glasses with ruby liquid. Turning, she gave Lizbet a full glass and Matias the stink-eye.

He understood her perfectly, and gave up his seat. He settled on the floor beside Kudo while Mawmaw leaned back into the rocker he'd just abandoned. She sipped her drink. "I don't suppose you heard about the trouble the fishery department is giving your Uncle Joe."

"No, Mawmaw." Matias gave Lizbet a sympathetic glance. "But Lizbet wants to learn about the Ollos Verdes, not Uncle Joe."

"Ah." Mawmaw rocked back in her chair. "That's right. It's a long story."

Matias gave Lizbet a questioning look before answering. "We want to hear it."

"Well, many moons ago, the world was made of two equal parts," Mawmaw began. "Animals lived in the water and people lived in a sky full of fertile fields, soaring mountains, and flower-filled valleys. One day, a Sky Child grew weary and fell asleep beneath the spreading branches of an apple tree. She slipped down a hole. Frightened, she wrapped her arms around the tree and it too fell through the sky.

"She called for help and fortunately for her, two swans were swimming in the water-world below. They rose to save her. Spreading their wings, they formed a soft nest for the girl to lie upon. 'What can I do now?' the girl asked. 'Can you return me to the sky world?'

"But the birds were frightened to fly so close to the sun. 'We'll take you to Big Turtle,' said one swan. 'He knows everything,' said the other.

"Big Turtle listened to the girl's story of a world with fertile land, tall mountains, and flower-filled fields.

"'If we can get some soil, we can create our own earth of land, sky, and water,' Big Turtle said.

"'But where can we find the soil?' Swan asked.

"''Tis below the water,' Big Turtle told them. 'We must dig deep.'

"Otter, Beaver, and Muskrat argued over who would go.

"'I'm the fastest,' said Otter.

"'But I'm the strongest,' said Beaver.

"'But I can swim the farthest,' said Muskrat.

"A little toad popped out of the water. 'I'll go. I can dive very deep.'

"The other animals laughed and mocked.

"'You're too small,' said Beaver.

"'You're too ugly,' said Otter.

"'You're too slow,' said Muskrat.

"'Hush!' Big Turtle said in a loud voice. 'We are all

equal, and we're all able to do our best. We will need the efforts of all.'

"The vain Otter smoothed his glossy fur, took a deep breath, and disappeared into the water. Beaver slapped his tail against the water before diving in. Muskrat followed. One by one they returned, gasping for air.

"'It's too deep,' said Otter.

"'It's too dark,' said Beaver.

"'No one can dive so deep,' said Muskrat.

"'I will go,' said Toad, before she sucked in a deep breath and disappeared beneath a wave.

"'We will never see her again,' said Otter.

"'She will die from bravery,' said Beaver.

"'She will surely drown,' said Muskrat.

"Moments later, Swan pointed at bubbles breaking the water's surface. Toad's ugly face appeared. She spat a mouthful of soil onto Big Turtle's back before sinking to the bottom of the sea.

"Big Turtle commanded all the creatures to rub the soil into his shell. The seeds of grain sprouted and grew and grew until a large island was formed. It grew into the world as we know it today.

"Eventually, the sky people noticed and grew envious. More and more fell from the hole in the sky to join our world. But only the descendants of the first Sky Child are the Earth's people. They are the Ollos Verdes—the green-eyed ones. Only they can converse with the Earth and its creations."

Slowly, Mawmaw raised her drink to her lips. "'Tis but

a legend, more pleasing to those with green eyes than to those of us whose eyes are the color of the soil."

"It's true, you know," Kudo whined.

"But how can the whole world be on the back of a turtle?" Lizbet asked.

"They say when the turtle moves, the earth quakes." Mawmaw raised her glass and peered into the liquid as if it had answers.

Matias laughed. "Well, that explains a lot."

Mawmaw frowned at him. "Do not mock what you cannot understand."

Matias opened his mouth as if to argue, but closed it again, and shook his head.

Lizbet took a swallow from her glass. Her vision clouded, and a memory danced before her eyes. It was Rose—the woman she'd known as Daugherty, her birth mom. She was laughing, and the sound filled Lizbet's head, making her ears ring. When the memory faded, sadness washed over her. She stared into the wine for a moment before taking another swallow. This time she saw Rose chattering with a squirrel perched on her shoulder. Again, the memory faded too soon.

"This juice..." Lizbet began. "What is it?"

"It's not alcoholic," Matias assured her. "I don't want your mom or grandmother to think I've been slipping you booze."

"I figured that, but... it's good."

Mawmaw beamed. "You like it, yes?"

"Very much. It's... dangerously good. Do you make it yourself?"

"Yes. It's an old recipe." She spat angrily. "That Igasho winery thought they could steal our brew! They are phonies!"

"My mom makes something like this. I guess you would call her a phony, too. It's good, but it's not..." She searched for the right word, but gave up and took another sip. This time she was young, younger than she thought she could possibly remember, and running through a field, her dog Emerson by her side. Grief, sudden and intense, ripped through her for her lost dog.

"It toys with your mind, no?" Mawmaw smiled and took a long swallow.

"What happens when you drink it?" Lizbet asked Matias.

He swirled the glass. "I don't know what you mean."

"Well," she shot Mawmaw a questioning glance, "what do you see?"

"The same things I always see." Matias frowned at her and then his glass.

"Here, try mine." Lizbet shoved her cup at him.

He raised an eyebrow, took the drink, sipped and swallowed. Licking his lips, he smiled at her. "I see you."

Lizbet swung back to Mawmaw. "Can I have your recipe?"

Mawmaw blanched. "No. It is a family recipe. It is only for Magena."

"But Mawmaw, we think Lizbet might be one of us."

Mawmaw firmly shook her head. "No! Might be is not the same as rightfully."

Lizbet bounced to her feet. "This winery. I want to try their wine."

Matias laughed. "You'll have to wait until you're twenty-one."

She blew out a breath when she realized he was right and fixed him with a steady stare.

He took the hint. "We need to go, Mawmaw." He climbed to his feet and bent to give his grandmother a farewell kiss.

"It was lovely to meet you," Lizbet said, taking Mawmaw's hand.

"Tell Grandpa and Uncle Joe hey for me," Matias said as he waved goodbye.

The wind whipped through the alleyways between the buildings, tossing leaves and torn bits of the wine's packaging labels and carrying the scent of wild blackberries. The Igasho Winery consisted of a collection of wood-framed buildings. The humming vats provided background noise. In the distance, the Cascade Mountains loomed over the acres of blackberry bushes. Declan found it hard to believe that all this now belonged to him.

Beside him, Gloria radiated with pleasure. It didn't seem to bother her that she wasn't the benefactor. He watched her out of the corner of his eye while Holbrook St. James droned on about the winery's profitability.

"Now, just to be clear," Gloria said, "since everything is Declan's, Godwin—should he resurface—can have no claim on it. Is that correct?"

Cabriolet cleared his throat and stepped forward. "Yes, that's correct."

The accountant, Mr. St. James, frowned at the attorney, clearly annoyed at being interrupted. St. James looked as if he'd researched all the stereotypes of accountants and glommed them all. Slicked-back hair, thin tie, white button-down shirt, pencil neck—Declan could easily imagine him sitting at a desk, punching numbers into a calculator, and humming delightedly as he counted money.

"Now, exactly how many acres are there?" Gloria asked.

St. James murmured a reply.

"We're not selling it," Declan spoke up.

Gloria cast him a surprised look. "Well, maybe not right away..."

"Not at all." The forcefulness in Declan's voice surprised even him.

"Goodness, Declan," his mom said. "I didn't even think you were paying attention and now you're saying you want to keep this place? You can't run a winery."

"Not right now, but that doesn't mean I want to sell it."

"What are you going to do with it?" His mom folded her arms and pinned him with her best mom-glare.

"It runs itself, right?" He turned to St. James. "We just met Mr. Eldridge, the manager. I assume running the winery is his job."

"Indeed." St. James looked pleased.

His mother much less so. "This would be a wonderful location for a condo complex, or one of those urban centers—"

Declan shook his head. "I'm not interested in developing anything other than blackberries."

"You don't know what you're saying," Gloria began. She stopped talking when she spotted someone, or something, over Declan's shoulder. Her eyebrows lowered dangerously.

Declan glanced behind him to see Lizbet and Matias rolling through the wide wrought-iron gates on a motorcycle. "Excuse me," he said to St. James and his mom.

Gloria grabbed and then held his arm. "This behavior clearly demonstrates how inadequate you are for running a business!"

"What behavior?" Declan could also lower his eyebrows dangerously.

"Your pretty little girlfriend shows up and you immediately check out."

"I'm not checking out." He scratched his chin. "I'm sorry," he said to St. James. "Go on."

St. James looked pleased and continued to drone.

Declan refused to look over his shoulder at Lizbet, but the temptation of her tickled like an itch between his shoulders blades. He had to admit that his mom was probably right. He knew nothing about running a winery, or any of his grandfather's other many businesses. His only job until now had been working in Neal's Nursery, watering the plants, hosing down the concrete, and spreading fertilizer. He hadn't even been all that good at it. But Mr. Neal was so nice he never complained, even when Declan occasionally screwed up.

"Declan," Lizbet said, coming up behind him. "What are you doing here?"

With her windblown curls, pink cheeks, and bright eyes, she looked beautiful. He could tell that Matias thought so, too. Why had she come here with him?

"I could ask you the same thing," Declan said.

"Remember how Rose, my birth mom, owned a wine business?" Lizbet glanced around. "I think this is it."

"You think your birth mom owned Igasho Winery?"

"Amazing, right?" Lizbet said.

St. James cleared his throat.

"Declan, darling," his mom said. "You should introduce your friends."

"Of course." Declan pushed his hand through his hair. "Lizbet Westmoor and Matias Hernandez." Geez, he hated even saying their names in the same sentence. Not that he hated Matias. He hated the way he was standing so close to her. "This is Leo Cabriolet, my grandfather's attorney, and Holbrook St. James, our accountant."

Cabriolet nudged him. "I'm your attorney now."

Declan flushed. "Of course." He turned back to Lizbet. "What makes you think Igasho Winery belonged to your mother?"

She shrugged. "It's just a hunch."

Gloria raised her eyebrows. "A hunch?"

Lizbet smiled. "You could say a little birdie told me."

Declan could practically see the animosity flowing between his mom and Lizbet.

"It would be simple enough to find out," Cabriolet said.

"But what would be the point?" Gloria asked.

"Indeed," St. James murmured.

"I'm trying to find out everything I can about my mother," Lizbet said.

"Maybe you should ask your bird friends," Gloria said.

"Mom!" Declan said.

"I'm sorry, darling, but—" Gloria glanced at her watch meaningfully.

Declan tried not to roll his eyes.

Cabriolet stepped forward. "Miss Westmoor, if you'd like, we could do a little research on the past owners right now."

"That would be wonderful. It's hard to explain, but ever since I learned my mom isn't my real mom—and

I don't really know who my father is—I'm burning with curiosity about my family and lineage." Lizbet gave the attorney her best smile, ramping up her beauty.

Declan tamped down his jealousy, and chastised himself, knowing Lizbet would never be interested in the middle-aged attorney.

Matias, though...

"That sounds like it could take a while," Gloria said.

"Yeah." Declan caught hold of that and turned to Matias. "If you don't want to wait, I can take Lizbet home."

Matias folded his arms and planted his feet shoulder-width apart, an impersonation of a tree that didn't want to be uprooted. "I don't mind waiting."

"Well, this is nice," Gloria said. "It's almost a party. I'd break open a bottle of wine, but sadly, you're all underage."

"Miss Westmoor." Cabriolet swept his arm toward the office. "Or should I call you something else?"

"You can call me Lizbet."

"Do you not know your real last name?" Cabriolet asked.

"It's complicated."

"If you need an attorney, I'd be happy to help."

Declan pressed his lips together, knowing he was being unreasonable and yet unable to shut down his feelings. If Lizbet needed help, he wanted to provide it. It killed him to watch her walk away with Cabriolet, with Matias trailing her like a puppy sniffing after a bone.

Cabriolet let Lizbet and Matias into a small office. Framed photographs of the Igasho Winery lined the walls. Cabriolet took a seat at the desk, turned on a computer and motioned for Lizbet and Matias to sit in the steel-framed chairs directly opposite him.

Lizbet's heart accelerated. Her thoughts went back to the day she'd discovered the safe in her mom's office. Of course, back then, she'd had no idea that Rose, the woman she'd known as Daugherty, had been her real mother. The papers and forms she'd found in the safe had meant little to her. Yes, she'd been disappointed and angry when they were stolen, but she hadn't realized until much later how much she'd actually lost.

While Cabriolet clicked on the keyboard, Lizbet sent Matias a quick look. He smiled in return, warming her, and she realized that he was a good friend. Almost too good. Would she want to hang with him while he rooted for his ancestry?

"Interesting," Cabriolet murmured.

"What?" Lizbet asked.

"It says here that Frank Forsythe bought the winery from the Moonlight Corporation."

"And who owned that?" Matias asked.

"The principles aren't listed." He gave them an apologetic smile.

"That can't be right, can it?" Lizbet asked.

Cabriolet pressed his hands on the table and pushed to his feet. "I'm sorry. This appears to be a dead end."

"No." Lizbet leaned back in her chair and folded her arms. "I refuse to believe that."

"Are you telling me that you don't know who owned the winery before Mr. Forsythe?" Matias asked.

"I'm telling you it was owned by the Moonlight Corporation." Cabriolet spoke slowly and distinctly as if they were foreigners who couldn't understand English.

Matias pointed at the computer. "Can I look at that?"

Cabriolet snorted. "I'm afraid not." He motioned to the door, dismissing them.

Sharing and giving are
the ways of God.
— Sauk

Chapter Seven

"You want the recipe of Igasho wine?" Declan blinked at Lizbet. "I'm sorry, but no."

She hadn't really expected him to give it to her, but still she had hoped. They walked side by side down the road, the sound of their shoes scrunching the gravel filling in the quiet between them.

"Your mom is, technically, the competition," Declan reminded her.

Lizbet lifted her shoulder. "I thought I'd ask."

"Why? So you can give it to your mom?"

Of course, she should have realized he would think that. What other reason could she possibly give? The truth? She wasn't sure if he'd love that, either. Still. She looked out over the neighboring pasture as the horses gathered near the barn. Why was it so much easier to talk to animals than humans?

She took a deep breath and plunged in. "Okay, when I went with Matias to his grandparents' house, his grandmother gave me some blackberry juice—"

Declan stopped walking. "You went with Matias to his grandparents' house?"

She nodded.

"Why?" Declan slowly resumed walking.

"Why not?" Heat curled in her belly. She should be able to go anywhere she wanted with anyone she wanted without being questioned by him or anyone else. Although, how would she feel if he went with Nicole to her grandparents' house? She'd be fine if he had a reason like she had. "Matias's mom is full Magena. I wanted to talk about the tribe. It's possible I might be, too."

"But you have green eyes."

"I know, but listen, she told me about the Ollos Verdes—or the green-eyed ones. According to legend, the green-eyed people are descendants of the first Sky Child." She told him the story.

He paused when they got to the large metal gates to Godwin's mansion and he pressed in the code on the security system. "Cool story, and probably even better if you're green-eyed, like you, but I don't know what it has to do with the Igasho wines."

The gates rolled open and Lizbet followed Declan through.

"I'm getting there. Matias's Mawmaw gave me some blackberry juice and it was... magical. Well, for me at least. Matias seemed immune to it. And she said that your winery makes something similar."

"But?" Declan paused on the front steps.

"But what?"

"That sentence sounded like it should have a 'but' following it."

"Most things have a butt following them." She slapped his behind.

His lips twisted as he tried not to smile. The door clicked after he finished typing in the security code.

"Don't you think this is sort of pointless?" Lizbet asked.

"Yeah, but sometimes with my mom, it's just easier to do as she asks."

"Godwin's smart enough to not be caught on the security cameras."

"She moved them. She's hoping he won't find them."

The house smelled musty. The plants looked sad and dejected, and a fine layer of dust covered the tables and piano. It was such a big house, it made Lizbet sad to think of it empty, unused and unloved. "I'll water the plants," she said.

"Why bother?"

"They'll die. They're dying now." She scowled at him. "You can't just let them die!"

"They're plants... They're not a mouse."

"They're alive... or at least they were."

He gave a bedraggled fern a concerned glance. "Lizbet..."

"What?"

"I don't want to argue with you."

"Good. We can take care of these plants now, or I'll take them back to Elizabeth's."

"Where you'll nurse them back to health?"

"Darn straight."

"How can you be so caring? It must be exhausting looking out for creatures, mawmaws, and houseplants."

"I don't look out for mawmaws," she said in a small voice as she stomped into the kitchen to find a water pitcher. "Mawmaws take care of themselves. But plants can't do that. Once you bring them inside, they become your responsibility."

"Yes, ma'am." He leaned against the doorjamb, watching her. "I'm going to start the security video."

She began opening cupboards, searching for a water pitcher. She screamed when she opened the third cabinet and spotted a mouse. She slammed the door shut when Declan dashed into the room.

"I'm okay," she said in a quick breath. "A bug flew out at me." She hated lying to him, but she didn't want another does-a-mouse-deserve-to-live conversation.

"And you let him live, of course."

"Of course."

Declan turned to go. "For the record, I don't blame him," he said over his shoulder.

"For attacking me?"

"For flying after you," he said without turning around. "I'd do the same thing."

She waited until she heard him turn on the security video in the family room before she pulled open the cabinet door. The mouse blinked at her. "There you are," she said as she drew out a piece of cheese from her pocket.

"This is provolone," the mouse said with a mouth nearly overflowing with food. *"I told you I wanted Gouda!"*

"You get what you get and you don't throw a fit," she whispered.

The mouse sat back on his haunches and folded his tiny arms. "Then I'm not going to tell you what I learned."

Lizbet scooped up the mouse and held him upside down by his tail over the garbage disposal.

The mouse squealed.

"Another one?" Declan stuck his head around the doorway. "Want me to take it outside and scare the cheese out of it?"

"How did you know he had cheese?"

"He's a mouse. Therefore, he likes cheese."

Lizbet thought about arguing with him, because even though she knew that not all mice liked cheese, this one did. "I got this." Swinging the mouse slightly as she walked, she headed outside.

"Tell me what you know, creature," she demanded as soon as the door had closed behind her.

The gathering clouds told her that the sunny streak was about to be broken and if she and Declan wanted to get back to the ranch dry, they would have to hurry.

"*Okay, okay,*" the mouse yelped. "*Just put me down.*"

"Not a chance. Tell me what you heard first."

"*At least put me upright. You're messing up my fur.*"

Lizbet held out her hand for him to stand on, but she kept her fingers curled and ready to squeeze if needed.

The mouse used both paws to smooth the fur between his ears. "*The dark-haired man returned. I heard him talking. He intends on taking Declan out.*"

"Taking him out?" Lizbet repeated. "What exactly does that mean?"

"*There'll be an accident.*"

"How? When?" She glanced over her shoulder at the den window where Declan sat at a desk before a computer screen. Her heart twisted. How could she protect him every time he got in a car? With a sigh, she moved behind a lilac tree so that if he happened to glance out the window he wouldn't see her.

"*I'm not sure,*" the mouse said. "*Something about the Festival of the River and Powwow.*"

Lizbet slowly nodded and set the mouse down on the back porch. "Thanks." She sank down on the bench near the Dutch door, discouraged. How could she protect

Declan? There were a dozen ways every hour of every minute for Godwin to "take out" Declan. Lizbet couldn't watch him twenty-four hours a day.

The only thing to do was make sure the police got Godwin before he got to Declan. But how? She was sure they were doing their best. But she could keep him from going to the powwow. She hugged her knees and propped her elbows on them, thinking.

Sometime later, Declan found her there. "No sign of Godwin on the videos."

"Really?"

He dropped onto the bench beside her. "You sound surprised."

"No! I mean, you had said you didn't think he'd dare show his face, so I guess you were right." This is what she said, but what she thought was, *Stupid mouse. Are you lying to me?* How could she protect Declan if she couldn't even trust her source? "Have you heard of the Festival of the River?"

"Yeah, I go every year."

She perked up. Maybe the mouse hadn't been lying. "You do? What is it?"

"It's put on by the local Indian tribes. My mom's broker has a booth, which I usually help man—you know, pass out fliers and such."

"But your mom's not selling real estate anymore."

He shrugged. "Yeah. We're not going to work the booth this year, but I still want to go."

"Why?"

"It's a big deal. Last year more than fifteen thousand people came. Come with me and you can see it for yourself."

"No, as a matter of fact"—she skated a glance at him—"I don't want you to go, either."

"Why not?"

"I have a bad feeling about it."

"A bad feeling?" He quirked an eyebrow.

She nodded. "I know you don't believe in vibes or... anything, but can you promise me you won't go?"

"No. I'm sorry, Lizbet, but just no." He gazed at her, his eyes earnest.

"Why not? I'm not asking for myself! I just want you to be safe."

"I'm going to go. I'm going to prove to you that there's no such thing as vibes. Your 'bad feelings,'"—he made air quotes—"are just your fears."

She huffed, but before she could say anything, he stopped her.

"You have to stop listening to your imagination. If Baxter were here, he'd tell you that you're letting your worries drive your actions. It's not healthy."

"I'm worried about you."

He bumped her with his shoulder. "I get that. Having Godwin take shots at us was scary. I love that you're worried about me, but you can't let that control your decisions. You have to move on and pick up your life."

She shuddered. "I imagine him behind every tree and lamp post."

Declan draped his arm around her shoulders, pulled her close, and planted a kiss on her temple. "I'm going to go to the powwow, and I'm going to be just fine."

"No you're not." She stood. "You're not going."

He pursed his lips and stared her down. "You're not listening to me."

"You are not listening to me!" She balled her hands into fists, trying to think. "If you won't go, I'll... What can I give you?"

He waggled his eyebrows.

She kicked his shin. "I'm serious!"

He laughed. "So am I!"

She stormed off the porch. "I'm going to stop you from going."

He marched after her. "I'd like to see you try." He caught up to her in two strides and grabbed her arm. "A minute ago, I thought I was about to convince you to have sex with me, and now you're leaving me?"

"I'm not leaving you." She stopped walking and placed her palm on his chest, liking the way she could feel his heart beating through his shirt. She leaned in for a quick kiss. "Please don't go."

He looked down at her, laughter in his eyes. "You're such a lunatic."

"Just humor me."

He lowered his head and kissed her long and slow. "Okay."

She pulled away. "Okay? Really?"

"Sure, you win. With me, you'll probably always win."

Relief washed through her and she hugged him tight. Leaning against his chest, she listened to the steady beat of his heart, praying she'd be able to hear that sound for years and years to come.

The next morning, when Gloria poked her head through his bedroom door, he rolled over and cast her a sleepy glance.

"Why aren't you ready to go?" she asked, clearly peeved.

"I'm not going."

"Why not? We always go."

"I don't want to."

"Seriously? You love the powwow."

"Not this year."

She folded her arms and glared at him. "What time did you get in last night?"

"Late."

"You were with Lizbet?"

He couldn't help but smile.

His mom blew out a breath. "You're leaving for Duke in two months."

"I know."

"So, I don't know where you think this romance is going."

"Right now, I'm not going anywhere."

"Well, that's obvious."

"Hey, teenagers need more sleep than adults, so let me do my healthy thing." He rolled over, put a pillow over his head, and as he drifted, he thought that maybe Lizbet really did know what was best for him after all.

"Now, why am I picking you up?" Baxter asked.

"Because my mom must have taken my truck," Declan said as he climbed into Baxter's Jeep and slammed the door. The Jeep shook as if threatening to drop the door.

"Why?"

"Probably because the battery in her Mercedes is dead."

"You tried it?" Baxter asked as he put the Jeep in gear. The car moaned as if it were being tortured.

Declan nodded.

"And where's your mom now?"

He told her.

"Don't you usually go to that?"

"Yeah."

"Then why are you here?"

Declan pushed his hand through his hair. "Lizbet. She asked me not to go."

"Why not?" Baxter flashed him a quick glance before easing the Jeep onto the highway. It lurched as it shifted gears.

"She said she had a bad feeling." He rolled his eyes. "Sometimes she's a crazy person."

"Good thing, too, otherwise she wouldn't be with you."

"Ha ha."

Baxter tightened his lips. "You know I'm in your camp, right?" The teasing dropped from his tone.

"Atheists united," Declan muttered.

"But you also know we're in a minority." Baxter gunned the engine and the Jeep complained with a slow shudder and groan. "And science has done its best to try and disprove intuition, but it can't. It's the reptilian brain."

"You're calling my girlfriend a lizard?"

Baxter grinned. "She's a hot lizard."

"Lizards are cold-blooded."

"Then she's not a lizard." He down-shifted as they approached a stop sign and the Jeep shuddered in response. "But she does have a reptilian brain. We all do. It's our subconscious. Scientists believe it's actually more in tune and in touch with what's going on around us than the logical side of our brain. And some people, people like Lizbet, are more dialed in than logical-thinking skeptics like us."

"Maybe." Declan turned his attention to the countryside flashing past the window. "Hey, thanks for picking me up. Mr. Neal needed me to come in at the last minute."

"Emergency in the vegetable aisle?"

"Something like that. Does it say something about me that both my boss and my girlfriend are loonies?"

Baxter slid him a grin. "Man, you better not let either

one of them hear you call them that. Besides, Neal is your former boss, right?"

"Yeah, but I said I'd continue to help out until he can find someone to replace me."

"Will you see Lizbet?"

His lips twitched. "She's definitely a perk. It's just—" He froze.

"Holy crap!" Baxter slammed on the brakes and the Jeep shuddered as it slid across the lane. The skidding wheels sent showers of glass shards into the morning air. Baxter gripped the wheel and fought for control as he navigated the Jeep to the shoulder and parked it behind a police cruiser with its spinning flasher lights.

Declan jumped from the Jeep and sprinted to the wreckage, taking care not to step on the burning flares. His truck lay upside down, the cab smashed in, the windows blown out, and the doors indented. "Officer! The woman driving this car?"

The portly policeman in a bright yellow vest held out his hands in a traffic-stopping motion. "Step back, boys."

"But that's my truck!" Declan gasped. "My mom?"

Baxter stood beside him, solid and steady.

Compassion flitted across the officer's face. "The ambulance left here about fifteen minutes ago. She's gone to East Side General."

Declan slid Baxter a questioning glance. Baxter answered with a nod toward the Jeep. "Let's go."

When a fox walks lame,
the old rabbit jumps.
— Oklahoma

Chapter Eight

Lizbet sang to the chickens as she scattered seed. They clucked around her feet, complimenting her on her aim and fluttering their wings. Lizbet enjoyed the chickens' company. They weren't naughty like the goats, or gossipy like the cows, or nervous like the sheep—not that Lizbet minded any of those creatures. She enjoyed them all. The pigs were always fun. They had a ribald sense of humor—always thinking up pranks to play on the other animals, but since they were much too lazy to actually do any of them, they just talked about them. Their outlandish and unfeasible schemes kept Lizbet wildly entertained.

"Hey, sweetie." Daugherty banged through the back door.

"Hey," Lizbet answered, glancing up. She didn't stop spreading the chicken feed until she caught sight of her mom's expression. "What is it? Is Elizabeth okay?"

"John just called." Her mom stepped up to the picket fence surrounding the chicken pen. "Declan's mom's been in an accident. It's pretty bad."

"Declan's mom?"

Today was the day of the powwow. Declan had promised he wouldn't go, but his mom must have.

"She was driving his truck."

"Why?" Lizbet wailed, clearly taking her mother by surprise. "Why would she take his truck?"

The chickens gathered around Lizbet, clucking their worry and commiseration.

"I don't know. Although it could have just as easily happened in her own car."

Lizbet doubted that, but she didn't say so. "Who else was involved?"

"There wasn't another car."

"What? She just slid off the road?"

"Who knows? Maybe she had to swerve to avoid hitting something."

"Like what?" Lizbet's voice was angry and clipped. "Of course someone else had to be involved."

"It could have been a deer."

Lizbet snorted. "You know it had to have been Godwin, right?"

"Sweetie—there's no evidence of any foul play. They'll have to wait until she wakes for anyone to know what sent her spinning."

"She's in a coma?"

"No, she's in surgery." Mom glanced at her feet before meeting Lizbet's gaze.

"What for?"

"Her hand was almost completely severed, plus she's broken several bones."

"Oh, wow." Lizbet leaned against the chicken coop.

Her mom patted her arm. "She's lucky to be alive."

"Is her hand going to be okay?"

"They don't know."

"Where's Declan?"

"He's at the hospital."

"I'm so sick of hospitals!" Lizbet said.

"Me, too."

"It must be weird for John."

Daugherty nodded.

"She's going to need a lot of help. Was it her right hand?"

"I don't know."

A selfish thought, followed by a wave of guilt, flashed through Lizbet when she realized this accident could affect Declan's decision to attend Duke.

Armed with a bouquet of roses for Gloria and a plate of cookies for Declan, Lizbet walked into Eastside General. The antiseptic smell hit her and the glaring white walls made her squint. Briefly, she relived the anguish she'd carried while her own mom was in a coma—back when her whole life had been turned upside down by the same man who, presumably, had tried to kill Declan and had nearly succeeded in killing Gloria.

So where was Godwin? Lizbet had to find him. She couldn't let him terrorize her life—or Declan's—anymore.

She found Declan in the family lounge on the third floor. He sat on the bright orange upholstered chair, his shoulders slumped, his hands clasped between his knees. She slipped into the chair beside him. "How is she?"

He glanced up at her with red-rimmed eyes and she realized he'd been crying. He shrugged. "She's still in surgery. Her hand was nearly severed, except for the main artery." He nodded slowly. "So that's good."

Lizbet rubbed his back in slow circles. "I'm so, so sorry." She swallowed. "I didn't know your mom would..." She caught herself.

Declan squinted at her. "How did you know? What did you know?"

"I told you—"

She recognized his pent-up rage. His anger must have been mounting with each passing moment.

"You told me nothing! Nothing you told me made any sense!"

"I saved your life. You would have been in that truck."

"Yeah, so I'm alive, but my mom nearly died." He stood and turned his back to her. "That doesn't make me feel any better."

"Declan, I'm—" She started to follow him.

He leaned toward her, his face contorted and furious. "How. Did. You. Know?"

"I don't know." She twisted her hands.

"I don't believe you. You must have heard or seen something. You must know something."

"You wouldn't believe me if I told you."

"Try me."

She rubbed her forehead, remembering her promise to the crows. She couldn't afford to anger them. Not now. She needed their help. One of their flock must have seen the accident. Swallowing, she came up with the only half-truth she could think of. "A bird told me."

Declan walked to the window and gazed out. "You gotta go. I can't even look at you. I don't know how you can make a joke right now."

"Declan, please." She laid a hand on his back and he flinched as if she'd stung him.

"I really can't. You have to leave before I say or do something we'll both regret."

Lizbet placed the plate of cookies on the chair where he'd been sitting and quietly left. She didn't start to cry until she hit the parking lot, but once she started, she couldn't stop.

"*Just apologize for being insensitive,*" Tennyson suggested as he snuggled up against her.

Lizbet stroked the cat. "It won't help. He wants to know how I knew, and if I go back on my promise to the crows, they won't help me."

"*They weren't much help anyway.*" The cat twitched his tail and tucked his paws beneath Lizbet's comforter.

"I just can't believe that there weren't any animals around at the time of the accident. I mean, it was right there at the edge of the woods. How could no one have seen it?"

She bolted upright as a thought occurred to her. "The only other time when animals hadn't been around was when there were wolves! Remember that?"

Tennyson rolled onto his back and stretched, clearly not that interested. "*You're forgetting something,*" he said. "*The mouse told you Godwin is responsible for Gloria's accident.*"

Lizbet's spine straightened. "Quick, what color are Godwin's eyes?"

"*How would I know that?*"

"Gloria would know... or Declan, but neither of them will want to talk to me, and even if I did ask them, they'd only think I'm that much weirder."

"*You think Godwin could be an Ollo Verde, like you.*"

"It makes sense, right? I mean, it's likely that he's my father. We know Rose's ex—presumably my father—was

searching for her. If Godwin has my ability, he could rally the wolves. They could be in league with him."

"Maybe, but why just wolves when there are so many other, superior animals?"

"You mean like cats?"

"Exactly."

The door rattled with a knock. "Lizbet?" her mom called.

"Yeah?"

The door eased open.

"Who are you talking to?"

Lizbet pointed at her open laptop. "YouTube."

"Ah." Her mom smiled, but her eyes were full of questions. "Declan's upset."

Lizbet nodded, and her eyes filled with tears. Again.

"I'm sure he's mostly upset about Gloria." Daugherty's voice brightened. "They were able to save her hand."

Lizbet couldn't speak.

"You should try talking to him again tomorrow."

"He won't want to see me."

"You should give him another chance. I'm sure he didn't mean..."

"But he did. You didn't see him. You don't know what he said." Her voice cracked, but she continued anyway. "You didn't see the way he looked at me. It was like he despised me."

"Sweetie, people say and do things in the heat of the moment that they would never—"

"That doesn't make me feel any better. People show their true feelings when they're upset. Those hot moments are the best representation of who we really are. Declan is... a skeptic. He thinks I'm stupid for being... intuitive. He scorns anything spiritual. That's who he is."

"Maybe for right now. Maybe you need to show a higher way of thinking."

"He hates me." Her voice quivered.

"No, sweetie." Her mom padded over to the bed, sat beside Lizbet, and nudged Tennyson out of the way so she could take Lizbet in her arms. "He just doesn't get you."

The tears welling in Lizbet's eyes began to fall in a steady stream down her cheeks. "He liked me yesterday. Or at least I thought he did." She sniffed and scrubbed her hand over her cheeks. "Mom, do you know what color Godwin's eyes are?"

Daugherty shook her head, her expression full of concern and a hint of laughter. "Why?"

"I don't know. Matias's grandmother told me a legend about green-eyed people."

"You have green eyes. Do you think you're a monster?"

"I didn't say anything about monsters!"

Mom planted a loud kiss on Lizbet's cheek. "Then what are you saying?"

Lizbet sucked in a deep breath, suddenly tired of feeling so alone and misunderstood. "I don't know. I'm just... tired and scared. Don't you think Godwin somehow caused the accident?"

Daugherty shook her head. "It was random. A fluke."

"I don't believe it. It's too coincidental."

She cocked her head and studied Lizbet silently for a moment. "How would you know? Why did you warn Declan not to go to the powwow?"

"John told you about that."

Lizbet hadn't asked a question, but her mom still answered with a nod.

"I've been so scared for Declan!" Lizbet burst out. "So sure that somehow Godwin is going to show up and ruin everything."

"Like he did before?" her mom gently pressed.

"Exactly!"

"Don't you see, sweetie? Godwin ruined your life once before, so now you're worried he'll do it again."

"It seems like a legitimate worry."

"Maybe, but you can't let fear ruin your life. There's a scripture that says not to take counsel from your fears. You need to have faith, even—no, especially—when you also have fear."

"I can't. I'm so scared of losing Declan."

"Yes, but... right now you're afraid you lost him and it's not Godwin's fault—it's yours."

The words burned in Lizbet's chest.

"I'm sorry if that hurts." Daugherty pressed another kiss on Lizbet's cheek. "Try to sleep." She patted Lizbet's leg. "Maybe you'll come up with some way to talk to Declan tomorrow."

Lizbet's days stretched out long and lonely, but her nights were filled with green-eyed wolves prowling through dark woods. She'd wake with her heart pounding only to find Tennyson snoring softly beside her and moonlight streaming through the window, casting shadows that hid only stretches of carpet. If she lay still, she'd hear the gentle breeze outside and the distant calls of owls proclaiming all was well.

Three days after Gloria's accident, she ran into Declan at the nursery. She shut off the hose and abandoned the herbs the moment she thought she heard his voice. Wiping her hands on her apron, she went to find him.

He stood at the counter talking to Mr. Neal, saying goodbye. She watched them shake hands. Mr. Neal slapped Declan on the back in a half hug. Declan caught her eye and his expression hardened.

She followed him to the parking lot. "You're quitting?" A light drizzle covered the cars and clouds darkened the morning sky to steel gray.

"Are you surprised?"

"It's not because of me, is it?"

"Not everything is about you, Lizbet."

She brushed her curls off her face and water rolled down her hand and soaked the sleeve of her sweater. "I'm sorry if I sounded flippant about your mom's accident. I didn't mean it to sound that way."

"Don't worry about it," he said through tight lips.

"How is she?"

"She'll need another surgery."

"When will she be able to come home?"

Declan shook his head. "I don't know. The doctors don't know."

Lizbet opened her mouth to say something, but Declan stopped her. "Don't tell me this is God's will or some other crock. I don't want to hear it."

"I wasn't going to." She blinked back the mist rolling down her face. "I know you're upset. You have every right to be."

"This has ruined everything."

"Especially for your mom."

He narrowed his eyes. "What is that supposed to mean?"

She stepped back, surprised by his reaction. "I was just being sympathetic."

"You think I'm more concerned about how this bunks my plans than I am about my mom?"

"I didn't say that."

They stared at each other for a few moments, then both blurted at the same time, "I'm sorry."

But the air between them remained strained.

"What can I do?" Lizbet said.

"Nothing. She'll need help when she gets home from the hospital, but like I said, I don't know when that will be."

She swallowed. "And your plans for Duke?"

"Are on hold."

"You're such a good person."

"Thanks. I don't deserve that."

"Why would you doubt it? Besides, neither you nor your mom deserved what happened."

He took a deep breath and closed his eyes, and his shoulders sagged. "I have to go," he said in a small voice. "But before I do, can you tell me how you knew about the accident?"

"I didn't know. Obviously if I had I would have told your mom not to go as well."

"So it was just a gut feeling."

She pressed her lips together while she thought of the proper response. "You don't believe in gut feelings."

"I didn't say that."

"You don't believe in intuition, or spiritual promptings, but do you believe in gut feelings?"

"More so."

"But not really?"

He shrugged. "There's some scientific evidence..."

"Scientists don't know everything, you know. Every question leads to another question. We think we're so smart, but really, compared to God, we're just—"

"I'm done." Declan clicked the fob to his dad's Honda and opened the door. "I'm not a believer. I never will be. You have to get that."

"I wasn't trying to convert you! I was just pointing out that there's a whole universe of things we don't understand!"

"Right. You're right. I'm beginning to see that you and I are probably not ever going to understand each other." And with that, he got in the car, revved the engine, and pulled away.

A starving man will
eat with the wolf.

Chapter Nine

Moonlight filtered through the tree's thick canopy, casting shifting shadows on the forest floor. The night sounds hushed as creatures took shelter in fallen trees and hidey holes. Squirrels quivered on high branches. Foxes cowered in their dens. A lone bobcat found refuge in a fern grotto while the gray wolf silently stalked through the woods, searching for something or someone.

Lizbet woke with a start, her heart hammering and her thoughts skittering between the two monsters preoccupying her thoughts: the wolf and Godwin. Could there be a connection?

She sat up when a thought occurred to her. What if Godwin was the wolf?

A werewolf.

She didn't believe in werewolves, monsters, or vampires.

But then, most of the world didn't believe humans could converse with animals and yet she did it every day. If she faulted Declan for being closed-minded about God, how could she be closed-minded about werewolves? But... come on. Werewolves? An image of a 1930s movie, *Werewolf of London*, flashed in her mind. She had watched it last Halloween with Elizabeth. They'd both laughed as Dr. Wilfred Glendon transformed from human to wolf, tearing off his clothes and howling at the moon.

Lizbet glanced at the smiling moon outside her window. It reminded her of the grinning Cheshire Cat in the *Alice in Wonderland* movie. The full moon played a role in every werewolf legend she'd heard of. She mentally counted back the days to Gloria's accident. Had it been a full moon? Was it possible a wolf had caused her accident? The police had determined another car hadn't been involved, but could she have swerved to avoid hitting a wolf? There hadn't been any animals around to witness the accident, and the only other time she knew of the animals disappearing was when the wolves had attacked Frank Forsythe.

And why would the animals attack both Mr. Forsythe and his daughter? Obviously, the Forsythe family must have something the wolves want. But what?

Lizbet threw back her comforter, crawled from her bed, and retrieved her laptop. Snuggling back against her pillows, she googled "full moon."

For centuries, pagans have believed a midsummer day holds a special power. Midsummer's Eve was believed to be a time when the veil between this world and the next is at its thinnest, and when fairies were thought to be at their most powerful. This year, the full moon and summer solstice will coincide with a rare strawberry moon.

Despite the name, the moon does not appear pink or red, although it may glow a warm amber. The romantic label was coined by the Algonquin tribes of North America who believed June's full moon signaled the beginning of the strawberry picking season.

Because the sun rises higher, the moon sinks lower, forcing moonlight through denser, more humid air. This potent combination creates the amber color, also known as the honey moon.

Thinking about honeymoons hurt, so she googled "werewolf."

The ancient werewolf legend predates written language and can be found all over the world in far-flung countries such as China, Iceland, Brazil, and Haiti. One of the first accounts comes from Greek literature when Zeus paid a visit to the Arcadian King, Lycaon. The king doubted Zeus's omnipotence and sought to trick him. He killed Zeus's son, Nyctimus, cooked up his flesh, and served it as the main dish at a banquet. Furious, Zeus resurrected his son before punishing Lycaon by turning him into a werewolf, and cursing him with a voracious hunger for human flesh.

None of this made her feel any better. After turning off her computer, she lay back against her pillows, stared at the ceiling, and tried to piece together a strategy. She had exactly two weeks to come up with a plan to capture and destroy a werewolf.

With the three-hundred dollars she'd borrowed from Elizabeth's honey pot, Lizbet crossed the pasture that separated her grandmother's ranch from the Hernandez's property. The morning sun skimmed the tops of the trees. It was early, but she knew Matias and his family would be awake. The sheep called baa baa as she ducked through the fence surrounding the Hernandez farm. She found Matias outside the barn.

He wore low-slung jeans, a pair of steel-toed boots, leather gloves, and not much else as he loaded lumber into the back of a pickup truck. He straightened when she called his name. His face registered surprise.

"Good morning," she said, biting her lip. "I've come to buy the motorbike you told me about."

"Really?"

She nodded.

He rocked back on his heels and studied her. "No. I don't think so."

"Why not?"

"Because you don't know how to drive it."

"But I've been on one. It didn't seem hard."

"It's dangerous. And you're small."

Lizbet rose to her toes, realized what she was doing, and came back to earth. "What does that have to do with anything?"

"You weigh like nothing. It takes a lot of strength of maneuver a bike."

"Didn't you say you started riding it when you were a kid?"

"Yeah, but I'm a guy."

"What difference does that make? Engines aren't sexually exclusive! But from this conversation, I would say that you are."

Matias grinned. "I don't think that means what you think it does." He held up his hand to stop her outburst. "What I meant was, I probably outweighed you even when I was eight."

"So what?"

"Look, I'll give you the bike—"

"You'll sell me the bike."

"But not until I'm sure you won't kill yourself on it first."

"What does that mean?"

"I'll teach you how to ride it."

"Mmm, okay. When?"

Matias frowned at his stack of lumber. "I have to check out the fences and make repairs."

"I can help."

"Really?"

"Sure. It'll be faster and besides, it'll prove to you I'm a lot stronger than I look."

But by the end of the day, Lizbet's arms and legs ached so badly from toting and hammering railing, she could hardly balance the motorbike. It didn't help that Matias insisted on sitting behind her and he weighed a ton.

"I really think this will be easier without you," she complained as she straddled the bike.

"Not a chance," Matias said. "There's no way I'm going to have to face your grandmother and tell her I watched you kill yourself on my motorbike."

"My motorbike."

"My motorbike. You haven't earned it yet."

"Or paid for it."

"I'm not selling it to you."

"Then what am I doing here?" Lizbet moved to climb off.

"I'm giving it to you—after I know you know how to drive it."

Lizbet sat back down.

Matias put his hands beside hers on the handlebars. "This is how you shift." He twisted the gear. "Do you know how to drive a car?"

"It's on my to-do list."

Matias blew out a sigh and it fanned Lizbet's neck. "Okay, you start it first. When the engine revs you'll see it on this monitor. But don't try looking at it. You gotta keep your eyes on the road."

"That's dumb. Why is it there if I'm not supposed to look at it?"

"It'll become instinctive. You'll hear it. But until then, I'll tell you when to change gears."

She twisted so she could see his face. "You believe in instinct, right?"

"Sure. Everyone does."

"But not everyone believes in intuition."

"Most people do."

"Do you believe in God-given abilities?"

"Sure."

"And God? Do you believe in God?"

He looked a little taken aback, but he didn't flinch. "Yes. I think everyone does. Even those who claim they don't."

Smiling, she turned to face forward. "I agree with you."

"Why?"

"Do you believe in werewolves?"

He laughed. "No."

"Okay, me neither."

"What does that have to do with anything?"

"It's just good to know."

She felt him laugh.

"Can we get back to the riding lesson?" His breath tickled the back of her neck.

"Of course," she said as she turned the ignition and the bike roared to life.

After three days of lessons, Matias gave her the bike. It was rusty-red with a cracked leather seat and worn-out tires, but she loved it. The first place she drove it was Eastside General Hospital. After stopping by the florist in the lobby and picking up a bouquet of flowers, she asked for directions to Gloria's room.

Hospitals still made her sad and anxious, but she straightened her shoulders and made her way up the elevator and down the hall of the third floor.

Gloria looked surprised to see her, but her expression softened when she saw the bouquet of flowers.

Lizbet caught sight of the roses she'd brought earlier and her heart twisted. Things had been so different then between her and Declan. Or at least she'd thought they were. That day had been the beginning of the end for them and she hadn't even seen it coming. Until then, she had thought—hoped—that she and Declan would always be together. Sure, she had known he was going to Duke, but she hadn't thought that meant he was leaving her emotionally.

"Lizbet!" Gloria brightened. "It's so nice of you to come by!"

It occurred to Lizbet that Gloria was lonely, despite all the bouquets of flowers on her windowsill.

"I wanted to see how you are." Lizbet came into the room, took a seat in a plastic chair beside the bed, and pulled off her backpack. Trying not to stare at Gloria's bandaged hand, she unzipped the bag and pulled out a plastic container full of oatmeal cookies. "And my grandmother sent you these."

Gloria made an effort to take them with her right hand, but then remembered and dropped her hand back to the bed and winced.

"I'll just put them here," Lizbet said as she placed them on the bedside table. "Would you like one?"

Gloria shook her head and looked defeated. "Not right now, but maybe later. I'm still learning how to feed myself with my left hand. It's not pretty."

"I'm sure you'll get the hang of it soon."

"I'm too embarrassed to eat in front of anyone."

"Even Declan?"

She nodded. "Even Declan. I'm sure he told you about the tomato soup incident."

"We're not really speaking right now."

Gloria blinked in surprise. "He hasn't told me that!"

An awkward silence fell. After a moment, Lizbet said, "We're just really different people."

"But that shouldn't stop you from being together." Gloria scooched up. "Listen, I'm not pretending to be an expert. I had two disastrous marriages and the second was worse than the first, which means that there better not be a third, because if it followed suit, it would be a doozy." Her attention wandered to the flowers on the sill, making Lizbet itch with curiosity to know who had sent what. "But I do know that Declan cares for you."

"And I care for him, but that's not why I'm here." She inched forward. "Did Declan tell you that I made him promise me that he wouldn't go to the powwow?"

"No, he didn't. What's that about?"

"It was a gut feeling. I can't explain it, but I just knew something bad would happen if he went. Then you took his truck and..." She waved at the hospital bed. "It's sort of freaked me out."

Gloria looked pale and shaken. "I can understand that," she said in a quiet voice. "What sort of bad feeling?"

"Call it premonition or a prompting..." She picked at a loose thread on her sweater for a moment before looking up with a sad smile. "Turns out, Declan doesn't believe in that sort of thing."

"No," Gloria said slowly, "but I'm glad he listened to you."

"You are?"

"Of course. I would much rather lose a hand than a son."

"Can you tell me what happened?" Urgency rang through Lizbet's voice. "I'm dying to know."

"Some sort of animal jumped in front of the car."

"Like a cow?"

"No. It was like a dog, but bigger. It reminded me of *The Hound of the Baskervilles*. Are you familiar with Sherlock Holmes?"

"Somewhat. Are you sure it wasn't a wolf?"

Gloria dropped her voice to a whisper. "It could have been a wolf, but that sounds crazy, right? I mean, a wolf killed my father and his nurse! I'm afraid if I claimed that a wolf ran me off the road, people wouldn't believe me. Does it make sense that wolves are out to destroy the Forsythe family?"

It might not make sense to everyone else, but it made perfect sense to Lizbet.

Her next stop was the University of Washington. She had an appointment with Dr. Madison, a professor of legends and mythology. Her legs and arms still felt wobbly from all the motorbike lessons and fence repairing as she climbed the four flights to his office.

She glanced through the ajar door. A large desk covered with haphazardly stacked papers sat in front of the window. Jammed-full bookshelves lined the walls.

A girl with a diamond stud in her nose and an armful of papers walked past. "If you want to wait for Dr. Mad, I'm sure he'll be right back. According to his schedule, his office hours should have started fifteen minutes ago."

"I have an appointment," Lizbet said.

"Yeah, but Dr. Mad doesn't run on people time. He lives by his own internal clock."

"I can wait," Lizbet said.

The girl cocked her head, trying to read Lizbet. "Are you a student? I don't remember seeing you around the Humanities building."

"No. Well, yes. I guess I'm a student of life, but I'm not attending the University of Washington."

The girl laughed. "Good answer. I think Dr. Mad will love you."

"He won't think I'm wasting his time? Because I'm not a student?"

"But you just said you are. You're a student of life!" And with that, the girl turned and left, leaving Lizbet alone in Dr. Mad's office.

She wandered over to the shelves. *Vampire Vanities*, *Ghosts of Chance*, and *Paranormal Paradigms* were just some of the books on the shelves. Mingled among the books were alien-looking tools and devices, wooden puzzles, and propped-up photographs, mostly of a middle-aged woman with weather-beaten skin and gray-streaked blond hair who wore an ever-present pair of binoculars strung around her neck.

"Hallo there!"

Lizbet twisted to see a small man with a pair of glasses perched on the end of his nose. He dressed like a living, breathing professor cliché with a beige sweater with leather patches on the elbows over a burgundy flannel shirt, navy corduroy pants, and a pair of loafers. He regarded Lizbet. "Casey tells me you are a student of life?"

"Well, yes."

He moved around the desk, settled into his chair and waved at Lizbet to take a seat. "What exactly does that mean?"

Lizbet sat on the edge of the upholstered chair. "It means I have some questions about werewolves."

Dr. Madison's fingers formed a steeple. "Is that so? Why?"

She hadn't been expecting that question.

"My grandmother has a ranch, and well, it wasn't that long ago when wolves used to be a problem around here, right?"

He pushed his glasses farther up his nose. "You're curious about the Forsythe murder, aren't you?"

She sat back, surprised. "I haven't heard it called that."

"What, murder?"

She nodded.

"Does that term offend you?"

"No, I'm just surprised. I guess I thought that animals attacked and only humans could murder."

"Ah. Interesting semantics—is it not?" He found a rare empty spot on the desk and drummed his fingers. "You're saying that animals are incapable of murder because they have no forethought. Therefore, they attack. Only people, who are scheming and sly, can premeditate murder."

"I don't think that's what I was saying..." She knew for a fact that many animals could scheme and plot as well, if not better, than some humans. She scooted back to the edge of her seat. "You teach mythology, right?"

"Yes."

"So you must have studied werewolves."

He nodded. "Yes."

"What can you tell me about them?"

"A great deal."

"So—will you?"

He glanced at his watch. "I would love to chat with you, but I think we'd both be better served if you took my class."

"But I'm not a student here."

"Hmm. That's a pity." He began to shuffle his papers as if he were looking for something much more important than talking to Lizbet.

Lizbet bounced to her feet. "If you weren't going to talk to me, why did you agree to meet me?"

He glanced up, surprised. "But we have been talking, yes?"

"Yes, but you haven't told me anything I want to know!"

"And you think that's my fault? You want to know about werewolves, but you haven't asked me anything other than for information."

Lizbet sat back down, hard, and stared at him.

He stared back.

Her mind raced with questions and she picked one. "Do werewolves only come out when there's a full moon?"

"The infantile, yes."

"The infantile?"

He nodded.

"You mean the young?"

He leaned his head to the side. "Young as in being new to the Lupine state."

"So those who have recently turned..."

He beamed at her. "Now you're cooking."

"So you're not born a werewolf."

He leaned forward and braced his elbows on the desk.

"There's no such thing as werewolves," he reminded her with a twinkle in his eye.

"Right, but hypothetically," she corrected herself, "according to legend, are werewolves born—is it a hereditary condition—or are they somehow created, like a virus?"

"I think you're looking for another V word." He waited for a second, before saying, "Vampire. You want to know if humans turn into werewolves the same way humans are turned into vampires."

She scrunched her forehead. "I'm not sure."

"And conversely, if humans can be turned into werewolves, you want to know if werewolves can be turned back into humans."

"Those are really good questions."

"You want to know if someone is doomed to spend eternity as a monster."

"I guess I do. Yes. That's what I want to know."

"Well, then I can't help you."

"What?" Her voice squeaked.

"The best I can do is give you some historical reference, but I have to warn you, you'll be disappointed. To my knowledge, a wolf once turned has never been the same."

"There's no such thing as werewolves," Lizbet said in a small voice.

"So they say, my dear, so they say."

"I don't want to know what everyone else says, I want to know what you think."

Dr. Madison rubbed his chin. "Then I suggest you enroll in my Monsters in Mythology class."

"I can't..."

"Can you audit?"

"I don't know... Can I?"

He smiled.

She considered him. "I guess I'll look into that."

He took off his glasses, revealing his green eyes. "I think that wise." He scribbled on a sheet of paper and handed it to her. "Here are some books I suggest you read before your first day of class."

Declan found Lizbet sitting by herself outside the academic advisor's office. Longing ripped through him, but he tamped it down with memories of their last few conversations. He'd behaved badly, and yet, maybe it had been for the best. They were a poorly matched pair. He was sane, and she was... who she was. He couldn't expect her to be anything other than her quirky self. But sitting there, flipping through a course catalog, her long dark hair shielding her face, she was beautiful. He knew if she looked up and smiled at him, he'd be lost all over again. It would be better if they didn't speak. If they didn't see each other. If he wasn't reminded of how she felt in his arms. How she tasted. The sound of her laughter.

She glanced up at him and caught him staring at her. "Declan?"

He found his voice. "What are you doing here?"

She showed him the course catalog. "I'm thinking of taking some classes."

"It's too late for you to apply."

"I know. But maybe I can take some night courses. Or audit the classes I like."

"Like what?"

Indecision rippled through her expression. She was going to lie to him, but he didn't know why.

"Humanities," she said.

"Humanities?"

She nodded.

"What are you going to do with that?"

"Study human... stuff." She swallowed. "Maybe I want to be a curator at a museum."

"You'd be good at that." She would be good at anything. "My mom said you came by."

She nodded.

Why couldn't he think of more than five-word sentences? He tried again. "That was nice of you."

"What are you doing here?"

"Checking things out."

She waited for him to elaborate, but he wasn't ready for that conversation. "I guess I'll see you around."

"Will that be okay?"

"Yeah." He took a deep breath, hugged his books to his chest, and turned away. "I'll see you."

Outside, he tried to remember what he was going to do before he'd run into Lizbet. The academic advisor. But Lizbet was in there. Could he act normal around her? Maybe. He'd bungled things so badly because she'd taken him by surprise. If he'd been prepared, he wouldn't have stumbled over his words and thoughts. Next time he saw her, he'd be coherent. Next time.

Oh please, let there be a next time.

"Do you want to go camping?" Lizbet asked Maria the next day while they assembled sandwiches for the quilting guild's annual luncheon and fundraiser.

Maria paused with her knife over the cucumber she'd been slicing. "Camping—you mean sleep outside in a tent and dig a potty in the dirt?"

"Yeah."

"Yeah. No." Maria whacked the cucumber into thin slices.

"Oh, come on! It'll be fun. I want to catch a werewolf."

Maria stopped chopping again so she could study Lizbet. "You're crazy, right?" She snorted. "And where did you learn how to catch a werewolf?"

"From the Internet." A spark of hope flashed through Lizbet.

Maria tried to hide her smile. "Let's suspend all rationality and suppose you really were able to catch a werewolf. Now what are you going to do with him?"

"Hold him captive until daylight when he'll resume human form."

Maria laughed. "Wow, you've really thought this through."

"So you'll come?"

Maria shook her head. "No. I'm not interested in werewolf hunting." Her chopping slowed. "Unless..."

"Unless what?"

"Maybe you could do something for me."

"Of course. I'd do anything for you."

"Get me a date with Baxter."

Lizbet's shoulders slumped. "I don't think I can. You know Declan is mad at me, right? If we were still together, it would be easy enough to arrange a double date since Baxter and Gina just broke up, but as it is..."

"Get me some alone time with Big Baxter, and I'll go on your werewolf safari."

Ideas flooded Lizbet's thoughts. "Alone time? That's different from a date. Alone time I can do." *Probably.*

"Get me some one on one with Big Baxter and I'm yours for the night."

"Done!" Excitement tingled through Lizbet. She had little hope in the ritual she'd found on the Internet, but it was doing something. Sitting around, worrying, and wringing her hands had never been her strong suit. Not

that hiding in the shadows was, but at least it was better than waiting for another wolf attack.

"When do you want to go?"

"Next Tuesday when the moon is full."

Maria laughed, picked up the tray of sandwiches, and headed into the VFW Hall where the ladies of the quilting guild were gathered. "Of course," she said over her shoulder. "I should have known."

Lizbet puttered the motorbike to Baxter's house with a pocket full of cold steak. She slowed when she spotted Declan and Baxter playing basketball in the driveway. Baxter was big, but Declan was faster. The temptation to watch Declan pulled at her. He moved like a dancer, fluid and strong. She felt his loss, and she missed him with a gentle ache. His absence had created a searing hole in her life. Countless times a day, she found herself wanting to share with him something that had happened. She would think, *Declan will laugh when I tell him*, or *what would Declan say about that?* And then she'd remember he wasn't speaking to her and laughing would be out of the question.

She gunned the engine around the corner, praying they wouldn't notice her. She drove on, mindlessly, wishing the clouds hovering on the horizon would open up and end the guys' game. She didn't mind getting wet, although her chances of meeting up with Tickles the Schnauzer in the rain were slim.

At the next intersection, she rolled the bike to a stop, considering her next move. She didn't want to hang on Baxter's street for hours waiting for a chance to chat with his dog.

He was a fussy little dog, vain about his fur, and particular about getting dirty. But he did like fine food, and Lizbet had pilfered a few steak bones from her mom's gig with the Rotary Club. An idea made her turn around.

She was going to need some tuna.

It is no longer good enough
to cry peace, we must act peace,
live peace and live in peace.
— Shenandoah

Chapter Ten

Tennyson, of course, didn't like being shoved in a backpack any more than he liked cruising around on a motorbike. Nor did he enjoy being Schnauzer bait, but he would do almost anything for tuna. Lizbet inched the bike to the corner of Baxter's street. She peered through the trees, hoping to catch sight of the boys' game. They were still playing, but as luck would have it, Tickles lay beside the court, head on his paws, looking bored.

Rolling the bike to a tree and propping it up, Lizbet took off her backpack and pulled the cat out. She'd rather do this without Declan nearby, but if she was lucky, he would never know she was involved. She hid behind a tree. "You know what to do?" she whispered.

Tennyson twitched his tail. *"Tuna. Every day for a week."*

Lizbet nodded and peeked around the tree at the game. Declan shot a basket and Baxter went for the rebound. Lizbet backed against the cedar tree and hid herself beneath its branches.

"And the good kind," Tennyson said with a hiss. *"Water-packed albacore. I don't want that oily, slimy stuff."*

"Water-packed albacore," Lizbet repeated.

"And it has to be Sunkist," Tennyson insisted. *"Not some generic brand."*

"Only the best for my kitty," Lizbet murmured as she set the cat down on the ground.

Tennyson arched his back. *"Wish me luck."*

"You'll be fine. He's a lazy dog who's missing his front teeth."

Tennyson wandered through the trees and onto Baxter's lawn while Lizbet watched from the shelter of the cedar's boughs.

Tickles sat up, his fur ruffled along his back. Tennyson waved his tail, sending his scent across the yard. Tickles bounced to his feet, yapping.

The basketball stopped thumping.

"Oh no. Keep playing. Ignore the dog," Lizbet whispered.

With a series of yips, Tickles bounded after Tennyson.

"Tickles!" Baxter called.

Tennyson tore through the grass with Tickles at his tail.

Declan said something to Baxter and Baxter responded by shaking his head. The dribbling resumed and the guys ignored the dog.

The cat scampered up the cedar to the lowest branch. Seconds later, Lizbet caught hold of Tickles' collar. She dropped the T-bone at his paws.

"*What's this?*" the Schnauzer barked. He bent to sniff. Then picked up the bone and began to gnaw.

"Would you like more?" she asked.

Tickles nodded as he worried the bone. Drool dripped from his beard.

"Then I need you to do something for me."

"*What?*"

"I need you to bring Baxter outside tonight when the sun sets. Can you do that?"

Tickles whined an agreement and plopped down at her feet to enjoy the bone.

"Lizbet? What are you doing here?" Declan pushed aside the cedar's boughs.

Baxter stood behind him, the basketball tucked beneath his arm.

"Looking for my cat." She nodded at the tree where Tennyson was perched, flicking his tail. "I thought I could coax him down with a steak bone, but your dog took possession of it."

"Sorry about that." Baxter dropped the ball, stepped forward, grabbed Tickles' collar, and hauled him back. Tickles skittered through the dirt, complaining.

Lizbet dropped to her knees and handed the dog the bone. "It's okay, he can have it now. He deserves it."

When Baxter released the leash, Tickles flopped onto his belly and concentrated on the bone while Declan picked up the ball.

"What for?" Baxter asked.

"For treeing my cat," Lizbet said. "If not for Tickles, I could have been chasing Tennyson for miles."

"He's already a long way from home." Declan sounded suspicious.

"I know, right?" Lizbet tried to hold her voice steady, but being around Declan made more than just her voice jittery.

"Do you need help getting him down?" Baxter eyed Tennyson with a tilt of his head.

"He won't come down as long as Tickles is here," Lizbet said. "Sorry, but it's true."

As if to prove her point, Tennyson hissed.

"You're right." Baxter elbowed Declan. "Coming?"

"In a minute," Declan said to Baxter, keeping his focus on Lizbet. "Do you need me to climb up and get him?" he asked once Baxter and Tickles headed back.

"I can get him," Lizbet said. "But maybe if you could catch him?"

"Merrow!" Tennyson complained. *"You are not tossing me around like a basketball!"*

Lizbet frowned at the cat, grabbed onto the lowest-hanging branch, and swung her legs up.

"Let me do it," Declan said. "Lizbet!" He reached for her ankle, but she kicked at his hand.

"Don't be silly. He's my cat," she said without looking down at him. A branch snagged her T-shirt. A waft of cold air blew across her bare belly, and she let go of the tree to pull her shirt down.

Below her, Declan sucked in a deep breath while Lizbet hoisted herself up into the tree and balanced on the branch just below Tennyson. "Besides, I'm already up."

"Yeah, now." He folded his arms and scowled at her. "I don't like this. You're going to fall."

"I'm fine." Lizbet scooched along the branch, drawing closer to Tennyson. Heat crawled up her cheeks, and to keep Declan from seeing it, she climbed, reaching Tennyson's level.

The cat eyed her before stretching out a paw and scratching her hand.

"What are you doing?" Lizbet cried as she struggled for balance.

"Helping you," Tennyson said.

"Help?" Lizbet cried as she hugged the tree with her thighs and tried to stay upright.

Declan dashed directly below her.

"I'm okay," she assured him as she regained her balance. Glaring at the cat, she lunged for him.

Tennyson hissed, jumped at her, and scampered up the tree.

Surprised, Lizbet lost her balance and her grip. She tumbled backwards and landed on Declan, knocking him

to the ground. Lizbet scooted off him, climbed to her feet, and extended her hand to help him. "I'm so sorry."

"Yeah, me too." He grabbed her hand, pulled her down, and rolled on top of her, pinning her. His face loomed inches from hers.

She held her breath, waiting for him to kiss her, or say something, but when Baxter crashed through the trees, Declan peeled away.

Baxter looked embarrassed. "I thought..."

Declan reached down to help Lizbet up. "It's not what you think. Lizbet fell."

"Yeah, and so did you." Baxter smirked. "You just won't admit it."

Lizbet brushed off her clothes, hid her flaming cheeks behind her curtain of hair, and wondered what had just happened, and what would have happened if Baxter hadn't interrupted them.

"Are you okay?" Declan asked her.

She lifted her eyes to meet his and nodded. "Are you?"

He rolled his shoulders and winced. "Sure."

Baxter elbowed Declan. "You going to get the kitty now?"

Declan ignored him.

"Tennyson!" Lizbet called.

The cat dropped down beside Lizbet's feet and meowed. She scooped him up.

Baxter watched, looking amused. "You should have done that five minutes ago."

Lizbet stroked Tennyson. "You're a bad cat," she said fondly.

Merrow.

"I'll walk you home," Declan said, falling in step beside her.

"No you won't," Baxter said. "We've got a game in Lake Monroe in twenty minutes." Baxter frowned at him. "Are you going to be able to play?"

Declan rolled his shoulders again. "I'm fine."

But Lizbet wondered if he really was, or if he, like her, had been more shaken by the fall than he wanted to admit.

The next afternoon, Maria dropped by Neal's Nursery while Lizbet was finishing up her morning shift.

"Are you almost off?" Maria asked.

Lizbet bit her lip and glanced at the clock hanging on the wall between advertisements for lawn seed and fertilizer. Her shift had technically ended a half hour before, but she'd been hanging around waiting for the deliveryman. She debated whether or not to share that information with Maria, although she did want to hear about her rendezvous with Baxter. "Let me finish watering these flats of alyssum and say goodbye to Mr. Neal."

Maria shifted from foot to foot, her attention wandering from the marigolds to the hydrangeas. "I don't get how you knew."

"Knew what?"

"Well, I went into the woods near Baxter's house, just like you told me. But I thought he knew I was going to be there. Turns out he didn't."

"So, he was surprised?"

Maria's eyes widened. "Of course."

"But pleasantly, right?"

Maria's cheeks turned the same color as the roses she stood beside. "I think so."

"So, what happened?"

"A bunch of people were there watching a movie, so he invited me in."

Lizbet shut off the hose. She really wanted to know if Declan had been there, but she didn't know how to ask without sounding pathetic. "Great. See, it totally worked."

"Declan was there," Maria said, sliding a glance at her.

Lizbet cranked the hose reel and tried to keep a poker face.

"Lizbet, oh good, you're still here." Mr. Neal poked his head out of the office. "Can I see you for a moment?"

Lizbet tucked the hose nozzle into place, whispered to Maria that she'd be right back, and headed for the office.

Mr. Neal leaned back in his chair and studied her with a puzzled expression. "Did you order Aconitum?"

Lizbet swallowed. "I did."

"Whatever for? You do know it's poisonous?"

"Yes, I know."

"We can't sell it. It's incredibly toxic."

"I'll pay for it. Maybe it was unfair to use the nursery, but I wasn't able to buy it any other way."

"But why buy it at all?"

"You know its more common name, right?"

"Wolfsbane." Comprehension flickered in his eyes. "My dear..." he began softly. "What happened to Declan's grandfather was a random, unfortunate affair."

"But grizzly. And totally preventable."

"Had he had wolfsbane on hand," Mr. Neal finished her thought. He stood and placed his hand on her shoulder. "Child, I'm afraid you don't realize how incredibly dangerous this plant is. I know it's lovely, but it's deadly."

"I understand that."

"You can't even touch it. The poisons can be absorbed through the skin and within a matter of minutes the heart will begin to fail."

"Mr. Neal, I assure you, I just want to—"

"You can't plant it in your yard as it will poison your cat! Not to mention any other animal that might wander too close."

Lizbet sank onto a chair. "You're not going to let me take it, are you?"

He gave her a stern glance. "I understand your fear, but I promise you, wolfsbane is not the answer. I'll take the cost out of your wages, but you will not be taking wolfsbane home."

"What will you do with it?"

His eyes got a faraway look. "I haven't decided yet." He gave her dismissive smile. "No hard feelings, I hope. I'll see you tomorrow."

Lizbet slowly took off her apron. She found Maria waiting for her on a wooden bench near the break room.

"Sorry about that," Lizbet said.

"What happened?" Maria stood and glanced at the closed office door. "He didn't fire you, did he?"

"No, of course not."

Maria waited for Lizbet to clock out and hang up her apron. "Then why do you look so beat up?"

Lizbet twisted her lips into a half-smile and headed out the door. "I'm fine. Tell me about the movie." *Tell me about Declan. Was Nicole there?*

Outside, the clouds that had been merely threatening a moment ago opened up. Rain fell in fat, heavy drops on the green and white awning sheltering the entrance.

Maria pulled her jacket's hood over her head and tied the strings. "It was dumb. But that's beside the point. I want to know how you knew Baxter would be outside at eight-thirty."

Because she couldn't very well say that all dogs, but especially Schnauzers, are fierce people-pleasers and therefore highly dependable and responsible, Lizbet shrugged and said, "Don't all dogs need to go outside before they go to bed?" She glanced at the raindrops bouncing in the parking lot and then the motorbike propped against the shopping cart stand. She'd never ridden in the rain before.

"But I didn't even know Baxter had a dog."

"Well, I did. His name is Tickles."

"I know that now..." Maria scratched her head. "So, you're telling me that if I have a thing for any guy who happens to own a dog, all I have to do is wait outside his house before bedtime?"

"Sounds stalkerish."

Maria acknowledged this with a nod. "Want a ride home?"

Lizbet shook her head. "I just remembered there's something I have to do."

"Like what?"

"I need several boxes of baking soda."

"What for?"

Tired of lying, Lizbet said, "So I can hide our scent from wolves."

Maria grinned. "So, when is the full moon?"

"Next Tuesday."

"What happens if it's rainy or cloudy and the moon isn't visible?"

Lizbet blew out a sigh. "Then we wait."

Maria and her mom could be heard yelling at each other through the open kitchen window. Lizbet felt bad about it, especially since she didn't know what they were saying to each other because she didn't speak Spanish.

But since she didn't want to spy on the wolves on her own, she didn't know what else to do.

"What are you doing?" Matias asked, coming up behind her.

Lizbet glanced at the plastic bag on the picnic table, grateful that it was opaque so Matias couldn't see her underwear inside. "The Internet called this 'clothes lasagna.'"

"Uh. Why are you making wearable pasta?"

Lizbet picked up the baking soda box. "I'm hiding my scent from wolves. Supposedly, baking soda can hide my scent from animals but I have to shower with it and douse my clothes with it."

"Wolves?"

Lizbet nodded. "Maria and I are going camping. Hopefully, we can spot the wolves."

"Why?"

"They make me nervous."

"Usually when something makes you nervous, you stay away from it. Not bathe yourself in baking soda and hunt it."

"True, but if I have proof that the wolves are still here and are threatening my grandmother's ranch, maybe I can get government help to get rid of them."

"So, you're not going to try and catch the wolves, you're just going to take their picture?"

"That's step one."

"What's step two?"

"That all depends on what happens on step one. It's possible we won't see even one."

"Even one..." Matias repeated. "You're hoping to find a pack?"

"Maybe. I think there was more than one at the Forsythe house, don't you?"

"I have no idea." He eyed the plastic bag speculatively. "That's not a very big bag."

"The less clothes, the less odor."

"Ah. Now I think I know why my mama and Maria are yelling at each other."

"Matias!" his mom called.

He grinned. "I think I know where this is going. I'll be right back." He paused on the back porch. "You okay if my clothes join in your lasagna?"

"Are you willing to shower in baking soda?"

He waggled his eyebrows. "Are you kidding? For the chance to be with you in the moonlight? Absolutely." He strode into the kitchen. Soon, his voice mingled with his mom and sister's.

After some intense wrangling, Maria banged through the back door. "I'm allowed to go only if Matias comes with us."

"That's okay, right?" Lizbet asked, feeling relieved but also a little worried about the scowl etched between Maria's eyebrows.

Lizbet dropped her voice to a whisper. "You didn't tell her about the wolves, did you?"

"No." Maria picked up her bag of clothes and baking soda and began to shake it as hard as she could.

"Good, because we're not going to really try and catch one this time."

"This time?" Maria's lips twitched and the lines between her eyes softened. "No, my mama doesn't worry about wolves. She's preoccupied with my reputation and what other people will think." Maria stopped shaking her bag, sat down at the picnic table, and propped her elbows up. "It's not really my mom's fault. It's my dad. He's so old-fashioned. He didn't want me to date—at all—until I was eighteen. Letting me go out at seventeen was like this huge compromise. And now he wants me to get married so he won't have to pay for college! How can he expect me to marry when I wasn't even able to go out until a year ago?" She blew out a breath.

"You don't want to get married, do you?"

"Not yet! I want to finish college, travel, work... Sometimes I worry I won't be able to do any of those things."

"Of course you will." She and Maria were both signed up for classes at the community college.

"You're lucky you don't have a father." When Matias pushed through the back door wearing an enormous grin and carrying pairs of boxers and shorts, Maria added, "or a brother."

"You don't mean that," Lizbet said. "For a long time, meeting my father was my most desperate wish."

"It's not now?" Matias asked.

"Now, it's a fear."

Matias pulled a plastic bag out of his pocket and stuffed his clothing inside.

Maria watched him with a frown. "That's all you're going to wear?"

"It's warm." He dumped a generous amount of baking soda into the bag. "You don't know that Godwin is your father," he said, meeting Lizbet's eyes. "Just because we think he's your birth mother's ex doesn't mean he's your father."

"It would be nice to know," Lizbet said.

"Why?" Maria asked. "I think it would be nice to live in a matriarchal house like yours. You don't even have an uncle or male cousins."

"You make us sound like an infectious disease," Matias muttered.

"I hadn't thought of that comparison," Maria said, "but I like it."

"You don't mean that," Lizbet said.

"Have you met my uncles and cousins? That's why I like Baxter—he's so huge, no one will pick on him."

Matias smirked. "That's what you think."

Maria picked up the baking soda box and shook it in Matias's face. The white powder dusted his skin and clung to his eyebrows, lashes, and hair. He roared, picked up his bag, and charged at his sister.

Maria yelped and ran while Matias sprinted after her. A few seconds later, they wrestled on the ground, Maria screaming and giggling while Matias tried to pin her down.

"Lizbet! Help me!" Maria called.

Lizbet didn't know what to do. The dynamics in the Hernandez family both baffled and intrigued her. She wanted to join in, but she didn't know how. The easy comradery Matias and Maria shared made her envious but also uncomfortable. Glancing around, she settled her gaze on the garden hose. She picked it up, turned it on, and pointed at the back of Matias's head.

He leapt off his sister with a growl, and moments later he had Lizbet beneath him, straddling her while the running hose created a puddle beside them. Maria tackled her brother, knocking him to the ground. The three of them wrestled in the sopping grass.

"Matias! Maria!"

The brother and sister froze at the sound of their mother's voice. She jabbered at them in Spanish and Maria and Matias both climbed to their feet and mumbled something in return.

Lizbet slowly stood and tried to brush off the wet blades of grass, but they refused to move. "I better go home and shower," she said.

"Here, take this." Maria shoved the box of baking soda at her.

Ten days and four surgeries after the accident, Gloria was allowed to go home. Declan helped her into a wheelchair, loaded the many flower bouquets onto her lap, and rolled his mom down the hall and out the door to her waiting Mercedes. A nurse carrying more flowers and Gloria's bags followed. He held open the door and waited for her to climb in. Gloria looked tired even though it wasn't even noon.

"Would you like to stop for lunch?" he asked before starting the car.

"If you want to pick something up, that's fine." Gloria wouldn't meet his eye.

He'd seen her attempts at feeding herself with her left hand, and it wasn't pretty. "Mom, you have to eat." Declan put the car in gear and headed for downtown.

"Not right this instant, I don't."

Declan drove in a tight-lipped silence.

"Where are we going?" Gloria asked. "This isn't the way home."

"I thought we'd go to Marciano's to celebrate." He slid her a worried glance.

"Celebrate what?" She sounded bitter.

"You're coming home!"

She made an ugly snorting sound.

"About that... I hope you don't mind, but I wondered if I could move in," he said.

"Why?"

"You don't sound pleased. If you don't want me to..."

"Declan, turn this car around right now. I'm not going to Marciano's and you're not going to move in unless... You know that you are always welcome at my house. I've begged you for years to move in, but now, I'm afraid, the answer is no."

"No? Really?"

"You are not going to take care of me."

"Mom! That's not what this is about." Although it totally was.

"The hell you say."

"Mom!" As far as he could remember, his mom had never sworn in front of him before.

"You are not going to be my housemaid!"

"Of course not. After all, I'm starting school in a few weeks." She bit her lip and tears welled in her eyes.

He reached over and patted her leg. "I want to stay with you. Dad is... dating Daugherty and it's weird."

"How are things with you and Lizbet?"

"Even weirder." He pulled up in front of Marciano's.

"Sweetie, I really don't want to be here. I don't have any makeup on, my hair looks like a rat's nest..."

"No one will care. You know that Lorenzo will be happy to see you."

"I care. And if you love me, you'll stop babying me."

Declan swallowed hard. "How about we try again in a few days?"

"See? This is what I mean!"

Declan put the car in gear and pulled out of the restaurant's parking lot. "I'm not following you."

Gloria jabbed her finger into his arm. "You're the kid." She pointed at herself. "I'm the mom."

He chuckled. "Believe me, I get that."

"I don't think you do. I think that since my accident, you've decided you wear the britches."

"Mom, stop. I don't want your britches."

She folded her arms and settled back against the seat, looking cross. "You bet your sweet bippy you don't."

"Do I have a bippy?"

"Everyone has a bippy."

"Sounds like a girl thing."

"See, you don't know everything." She looked like she wanted to say more, but she froze.

Declan followed her gaze to his grandfather's house. A large dark Land Rover stood in the driveway.

"Why is he here?" Gloria asked, touching her hair and adjusting her sweatshirt.

"Who is it?"

"That's Leo Cabriolet's car." She eyed Declan suspiciously. "Did you arrange this?"

Declan took his foot off the gas, allowing the car to slow. "No. I tried to railroad you into lunch at Marciano's, but that's about as devious as I get. I don't know what he's doing here, but you can ask him in about five seconds."

"I don't suppose you want to drive around the block? Maybe he'll be gone by the time we get back."

"I thought you liked Cabriolet."

"I do... I just..."

"Are we back to the makeup and rat's nest thing?"

Gloria responded by pressing her lips together. A wave of pity—an emotion he'd never before paired with his mom—washed over him. She had always been a force of nature in his life—a whirlwind that he couldn't control or manipulate in any way. He sometimes wondered if she'd been the same for his dad. She had been more evenly matched with Godwin—but that marriage, of course, had been a disaster. Mostly because Godwin was a psychopath.

Declan could see Cabriolet in the driver's seat talking on the phone. "I wonder how he knew you were coming home. You didn't tell him, did you?"

"I don't remember. But I've been so loopy and drugged up this week, for all I know I could have told him my weight and age."

Declan laughed. "And that would be bad?"

"Everyone has a different definition of tragedy."

"I guess," Declan said as he rolled the Mercedes into the driveway beside Cabriolet.

"Let me talk to him on my own, okay?"

"Um, sure. Do you want help getting out of the car?"

Gloria shook her head. "Do you mind taking my bags upstairs to my room?"

Declan smiled and waved at the attorney, gathered his mom's things from the trunk, and headed up the stairs. At the top, he considered the four empty bedrooms and chose the one overlooking the backyard for his own.

Lizbet smiled at the moon as she wrapped her sheet into a small roll and tucked a pocket-sized flashlight into her shorts.

"That's it?" her mom asked. "No sleeping bag or tent?"

"Good thing it's warm," Lizbet said, tucking her roll beneath her arm and heading down the stairs.

Daugherty trailed after her. "No fire? No food? No marshmallows? What kind of campout is this?"

"It's a wolf watching trip," Lizbet said without looking over her shoulder.

"I've heard of whale watching, but not wolf watching." She paused. "Maria and Matias are both going?"

Lizbet nodded.

"Do you want to take a gun?"

Lizbet hesitated by the back door. Using the arm that wasn't occupied with the balled-up sheet, Lizbet hugged her mom. "I don't want to shoot anyone."

"Is a wolf an anyone or an anything?"

Lizbet laughed. "Does it matter?"

"I bet it does to the wolves."

She kissed her mom's cheek. "Love you, Mom."

"Do you want to take my phone?"

Lizbet shook her head.

Daugherty planted her feet hip-distance apart. "I insist you take a phone!"

Lizbet slowly turned. "You know, a few weeks ago, you didn't even know cell phones were a thing."

"Thank you." Daugherty smiled and dropped the phone into Lizbet's outstretched hand.

Lizbet slipped the phone into her pocket. She crossed the lawn, crawled through the split-rail fence and entered the pasture. When she reached the shelter of the woods she pulled the phone out and turned it off.

We are all one child spinning
through Mother Sky.
— Shawnee

Chapter Eleven

The doorbell rang. Rufus ran to the front door, barking, but Declan didn't look up from his laptop. He had to register for classes and none of them were right. It seemed wrong to be studying organic chemistry when his mom had to learn how to use a fork with her left hand.

"Your friends are here," Gloria called. She turned off the TV, sat up in her chair a tad straighter, and patted her hair into place.

Declan glanced out the window. Baxter, McNally, Nicole, Hailey, and Carly stood on the porch. The girls all waved and smiled when they caught his attention while the guys tried to be cool. Declan pulled away from his computer and went to let his friends in.

"There's a full moon tonight," Nicole said in a singsong voice.

"You know what that means." McNally tipped his head back and howled.

Baxter elbowed McNally, sending the smaller guy off the porch and into a shrub.

"Hey!" McNally staggered out of the garden bed and brushed himself off. He played forward on their basketball team and what he lacked in height he made up for in aggression.

"We're going to play night games," Nicole said, flashing a smile at Declan. "Want to come?"

"Nah--," Declan began.

"Declan, go." His mom cut him off. "I'm tired of you hanging around here like a puppy who's lost his bone."

"I'm registering for my classes," Declan said, shifting his weight from one foot to the other.

"You already did that," Gloria said.

Declan heard the questions in her voice, but he didn't turn to look at her. "I'm making some changes." Changes he didn't want to discuss with her. At least not yet.

"How long can that take?" Gloria asked.

"You should come," Nicole whined.

"Without you, we're outnumbered," McNally said.

Hailey winked at him. "Do you really want to be responsible for the girls dominating the guys?"

All the girls were on the tennis team; athletic but not a serious match against the basketball players. Declan

smirked. "I think Baxter on his own could take you all on," he told the girls.

"Hey!" Nicole cried.

"Oh, yeah?" Hailey tried to push Baxter off the porch, but he didn't budge.

"What does that say about me?" McNally puffed out his chest and squared his shoulders.

"It says you don't need me."

"Of course we don't need you." Nicole reverted to her whiny voice. "But we want you to come."

"Declan, go!" Gloria demanded.

Declan cast a glance at his laptop. He had to register soon before the classes he wanted were snatched up by other late-to-the-party freshmen and also before he changed his mind... again, but... "Let me get my shoes."

Maria and Matias were just shadows waiting on their porch. Lizbet waved as she approached. Like her, they wore dark shorts, T-shirts, and sandals. Matias was chomping on potato chips.

Lizbet pointed at the bag. "You can't bring those."

"Why not?" He lifted the open bag to his nose. "They don't smell."

"Maybe not to us, but a wolf can probably smell them from a hundred miles from here."

Matias looked unhappy, but he rolled the top of the bag closed and left it on the patio table. He brushed his hands together as if he were washing them. "Let's go."

Maria balked. "Are you sure about this?"

Lizbet nodded. "We're just going to see if we can find them."

"That's not what you said earlier. You said you wanted to catch a werewolf and hold it captive until daylight to see if it will shift back into human form."

Matias lifted his eyebrows and laughed. "You said that?"

"Oh come on, you can't believe I was serious. There's no such thing as werewolves."

"You sounded serious," Maria said. "So serious I did some reading. Don't you think it's weird that almost every civilization has a recorded werewolf legend? Just think about it. Why would the Chinese and the ancient Greeks both have werewolves in their mythology? The two cultures couldn't have overlapped in anyway."

"You don't know that." Matias nudged his sister.

"But what I do know is that *that* is one creepy moon," Maria said, nodding at it.

"It's a strawberry moon," Lizbet said, linking her arm through Maria's and gently leading her across the lawn.

"A what?" Matias asked.

"Strawberry moon."

"Are there blueberry moons? How about huckleberry?" Matias joked.

Maria relaxed against Lizbet until they reached the edge of the woods. "Are you sure about this?" she asked.

"I want to see the wolves," Lizbet said, "but if you don't, I get that."

"She'll still have me," Matias chirped from behind them.

Lizbet would rather not spend the night alone with Matias. Not that she didn't trust him, but she worried what Declan would think if he found out.

He wouldn't care.

He wouldn't even know.

But she thought of how she'd feel if she learned he went camping alone with Nicole. It would hurt. And she was already hurting. But she had no idea what he was feeling. Or thinking. Or who he was seeing.

Maria heaved a big sigh. "I can't leave you alone with this doofus. I mean, what if you really did see the wolves?"

"Oh yeah, like we really need you to protect us," Matias scoffed.

"Three is better than two," Lizbet said, trying to keep the peace.

"So, why is the moon red?" Maria asked, obviously trying to infuse bravery into her voice.

"Supposedly, it got its name from Native American tribes because it arrives in June, when strawberry season is at its peak," Lizbet told them. "It's supposed to signal the time to pick the berries. In Europe, it's called a rose moon."

"Either way, it's a freaky color," Maria said.

Matias nodded. "Like blood."

Maria whirled around to slug her brother.

"Ow!" He rubbed his arm and glared at her.

Lizbet had to stop herself from rolling her eyes. Maybe bringing the brother and sister team had been a bad idea. "Guys, we have to be quiet. I bet the wolves' sense of hearing is a lot stronger than ours."

Maria wrapped her arm through Lizbet's again while Matias trailed behind them. As they walked in silence through the dark woods, Lizbet listened for chattering squirrels, hooting owls, or scurrying fox. She heard nothing but their own footsteps and the gentle swoosh of the breeze playing in the trees. Shadows shifted through the forest. The light of the strawberry moon hit the ground in gray splotches. The world seemed as lifeless and flat as a black and white photograph. A chill that had nothing to do with the weather crawled over her.

"In the forest dark and deep," Matias said in a low, gravelly voice, "do not wander, do not sleep."

Maria twisted toward him. "How many times do I have to hit you?" she hissed.

Matias met her hostility with a grin. "Don't worry, I'll protect you." He draped his arms over Lizbet and Maria's shoulders. Without his shirt, his skin felt hot and sticky. Lizbet flinched away. Maria pushed him.

He stumbled before catching himself. "What was that?" he asked.

"What?" Lizbet asked.

"I heard it, too," Maria said.

"Does everyone know how to play?" Even though Hailey was the smallest, she had somehow become the ringleader. She'd led them to the deepest part of the woods and paired them up into teams. "It's basically hide and seek in reverse. One team hides while the others search for them. Once one team finds them, they have to hide with the starting team until the last team also finds them. So pick a big hiding place." She winked. "Or if you want to get cozy, pick a small space. We'll shuffle teams after every round."

Declan ran a finger around the collar of his T-shirt and slid a glance at Nicole, his team partner. He now knew why they'd wanted him to come.

McNally picked a stick off the ground and broke it into three pieces. "The short stick goes first," he said as he turned around to adjust the three sticks in his grasp. He held out his hand to Nicole. "Ladies first."

She drew and Hailey followed. They compared their sticks, but they were similar in size. McNally grinned as Carly picked the short stick. "It's you and me, babe," he said.

Declan, Baxter, Hailey, and Nicole stood in a circle, held hands and counted to a hundred, the numbers falling from their lips like a chant.

"One. Two. Three..."

Declan tried to tell himself he was having fun, but he just wasn't feeling it. His thoughts wandered. Ever since his mom's accident, he'd felt as if the world as he'd known it had shattered. It was as if his life had been scribbled with marker on a sheet of glass and someone as a joke had dropped the glass and now he had to somehow put it back together so the scribbling still made sense. He had answers for the big questions: college, yes—but where? Was leaving his mom the kind or responsible thing to do? She had never really needed him before, but now she did.

"Fifty. Fifty-one. Fifty-two..."

Although, she would say she didn't. She wouldn't want him to readjust his life and dreams for her.

And if he was going to think about rearranging his dreams for women, he'd have to think about Lizbet, who he'd been trying to put out of his head for days. Weeks. It seemed like years. How had she become so significant in such a short time? He had to admit that he'd made her the star he guided his life by. She was like the center of his storm—the quiet refuge he desperately needed when nothing else made sense.

"Seventy. Seventy-one. Seventy-two..."

And *that* made no sense, because if anyone was confusing, if anyone could turn him inside out, it was Lizbet. Anger and frustration gripped him all over again. If she would just tell him how she'd known about the accident...

But maybe she couldn't. Maybe she really did pick up on vibes. Maybe she really did have a hyper-spidey sense. Chills crawled over his skin.

Nicole squeezed his hand, reminding him of the game. He opened his eyes and met her hopeful gaze.

Nicole was Lizbet's polar opposite: tall, blond, from a white-bread-and-butter, upper-middle-class family. They were opposite not only in their backgrounds and appearances. Nicole didn't have an imagination, and Lizbet was dominated by hers.

And she was right a spooky amount of the time.

Nicole tugged at him. "Come on," she urged.

He noticed with some surprise that Baxter and Hailey had already disappeared into the trees. He let Nicole keep hold of his hand, and she led him in the opposite direction.

"You're rethinking Duke, aren't you?" she said without looking at him.

"How did you know?"

"Makes sense, what with your mom's accident and everything."

He wondered if she knew the everything meant Lizbet. Even though they weren't speaking, the thought of being on the other side of the country from her tore him up.

"No one knows."

"Even your mom?"

"Especially not my mom."

"You think she'll try and stop you?"

He nodded. "She's so twisted. She fought my going to Duke before her accident, and now that she needs help, she'll insist I go."

"She wants you to live your dreams."

"I can still have my dreams. The UW is a good school. The crazy thing is I wouldn't have even applied there if she hadn't insisted earlier."

"Do you think she had a premonition?"

"No." His words came out harsher than he intended.

Nicole didn't say anything for a long beat of silence. "I applied to Duke because of you," she whispered.

"You shouldn't have done that."

She shrugged. "But I did."

"Nicole, listen..."

"Baxter told me you broke up with Lizbet." She spoke quickly, as if she was afraid he'd interrupt her.

"It's true, but—" He froze when he saw Lizbet wearing a pair of cut-offs and a black bikini top, standing in a shaft of moonlight. Two shadowy forms stood behind her. For a moment he thought he was hallucinating. "Lizbet? What are you doing here?"

Her gaze settled on his hand clasped in Nicole's and her expression turned hard. "What are you doing here?"

Matias and Maria Hernandez stepped out from behind and flanked her like bodyguards as if they needed to protect her from him. Matias wasn't wearing a shirt. In fact, all of them seemed scarcely dressed. What the hell?

"That's none of your business," Nicole said, her voice as hard as Lizbet's expression.

"We're playing a game," Declan said.

"Yeah, and we're sure to lose now," Nicole said.

"So sorry to spoil your fun," Maria said, her voice dripping with sarcasm.

Matias draped his bare arm over Lizbet's slim shoulders. Jealousy, hot and intense, flashed through Declan forcing him to close his eyes.

"Let's go," Matias said, turning Lizbet away. "Sorry we interrupted your game."

Maria faced him with her hands on her hips. "Are you sure you're all legal to play?"

"What does that mean?" Nicole asked.

"Declan's eighteen. Are you?" Maria shot back.

"It's not that kind of game," Nicole said through clenched teeth.

Maria responded by lifting one eyebrow.

"What's that?" Lizbet froze and pointed at a shadow running through the ferns.

"Is it a wolf?" Matias asked.

Lizbet squinted in the darkness. "I don't think so. It wasn't big enough."

Nicole elbowed Declan. "Was it Baxter and Hailey?" she whispered.

"I didn't see it," Declan admitted, "but if it's too small to be a wolf, it's certainly not Baxter."

"Maybe Hailey?"

"She's little, but she's still taller than a wolf."

Matias grinned. "Unless she's a werewolf."

Lizbet kicked him.

"What?" he asked, his voice full of laughter. "I'm just saying what everyone else is thinking."

"I wasn't thinking that," Declan said.

"Yeah, no one wants to know what you're thinking," Maria said.

And now Maria hates me, Declan thought. *As well as Lizbet.* This had to stop. Now.

"Lizbet, can I—"

"Tickles!" Baxter's voice boomed through the dark forest. "What are you doing here?"

"Tickles?" Maria's voice went up on octave. She ran after the sound of Baxter's voice.

The others trailed after her. They found Baxter kneeling beside his dog, ruffling Tickles' fur.

Hailey stood beside him, frowning. "We can't hide with your dog. He'll give us away."

"We'll take your place," Matias suggested. He still had his arm slung around Lizbet.

Declan imagined Matias and Lizbet pressed into some hidey-hole together and his gut tightened. He couldn't be there anymore. He couldn't pretend any longer. "I'll take Tickles home."

"No, let me," Lizbet spoke up. "There's an uneven

number. It makes sense for me to go. Without me, there's an even number of girls to guys."

"What? Absolutely not," Matias exploded. "I don't want to play this game without you."

"It's not that sort of a game," Declan growled. "And you're not playing with her."

Matias stepped forward, all laughter now gone from his voice. "And neither are you."

"Hey, guys, chill." Hailey stepped between them.

"No one needs to go because of the dog." Baxter folded his arms. "If you guys want to play, we can tie Tickles up to a tree. He'll be fine."

"He doesn't even have a leash," Hailey pointed out.

"I don't want to play," Lizbet said in a small voice, ducking out from under Matias's arm. "I'll walk him home."

"In the dark? Alone?" Matias asked.

"You're so sexist!" Maria exploded. "You're just like Dad!"

"I'm not sexist! I'm just practical. She shouldn't be walking alone in the dark." Matias skated a glance at Declan.

"Huh, guys?" Hailey tried to interrupt them.

"Look, the three of us will go," Matias said.

Maria glanced at Baxter. "I want to stay."

"You should stay, too," Lizbet told Matias. "That way there's an even number."

"Guys!" Hailey called out.

"What?" Declan asked.

"Tickles is gone."

Listening to a liar is like
drinking warm water.
- Tribe Unknown

Chapter Twelve

Anger, white and hot, zipped through Lizbet. "Tickles!"

Everyone began calling the dog. McNally and Carly emerged from behind a fallen tree.

"What's going on?" McNally asked.

"Tickles is gone," Hailey told him.

"You brought your dog?" McNally asked Baxter.

"No, he just showed up," Baxter said.

"Maybe he went home," Hailey suggested hopefully.

A howl tore through the night, silencing the group.

"The wolves," Matias said in a hushed breath.

"Wolf," Lizbet corrected him. "Just one, I think."

"Don't they usually travel in packs?" Maria asked.

Lizbet nodded, noting Declan's suddenly pale face.

"Tickles!" Panic filled Baxter's voice, and he took off after the howling. Declan, Nicole, Hailey, and Nicole followed while Matias, Maria, and Lizbet hung back.

"Will the wolves hurt the dog?" Matias whispered to Lizbet.

"Maybe," she whispered back. "They have to eat."

"Let's go home," Matias urged. "We wanted to find the wolves and we have."

Maria nodded in agreement.

"But I want to see if it's the same one I saw outside Declan's grandfather's house." Lizbet bit her lip, considering. Worry tightened her belly. Thinking about Tickles at the mercy of the wolves made her sick. "Do you guys want to stay here while I go and look?"

"Let's stay together," Matias said, linking his arm through hers. Maria took her hand and squeezed it.

"Did it hurt to see him with her?" Maria whispered.

Lizbet shrugged. Yes, but she told herself her own petty jealousies were insignificant compared to Tickles' safety.

"Forget him," Matias said, pulling her a smidge closer.

Weeks slid by and Declan made no effort to contact Lizbet. She learned from Maria that Tickles had returned

to Baxter's house, healthy and happy, the night they'd met up in the woods. Still, Lizbet began auditing Professor Madison's Wednesday night mythology class.

They met in an auditorium built for hundreds, but less than twenty students filled the seats. Intimidated, Lizbet chose a place in the back near the door. Professor Madison spotted her and winked. She gave him a small wave and her full attention.

He spoke without looking at his notes or the stack of books he placed on the podium. "As we discussed last week, in Greek mythology, Lycaon was a king of Arcadia, son of Pelasgus and Meliboea, who, in the most popular version of the myth, tested Zeus by serving him the roasted flesh of Nyctimus in order to see whether Zeus was truly omniscient. In return for these gruesome deeds, Zeus transformed Lycaon and his fifty sons into the forms of wolves.

"Now, what do we know about wolves? They're strong. Their senses are much keener than humans. Their society is more tightly knit than ours. They mate for life." He chuckled. "There are many wolfish characteristics that we humans should try and emulate.

"Trying to catch a wolf in any kind of trap would be a foolish waste of time. A wolf is one of the most vicious and bloodthirsty animals. Often, they simply kill as much as is possible, regardless of hunger and appetite. Then the wolf pack can tear the prey apart and eat at their own will.

Although savage, wolves are among some of the world's smartest and most perceptive mammals. They are found all over the world, and on almost every major continent of the Earth. This, perhaps in part, would explain why the werewolf legend is so pervasive.

"But does it really?"

Lizbet left the class in a daze. Her thoughts spun as she headed for the ranch, imagining wolves behind every tree. Lizbet rolled the motorbike down the drive, but nearly lost her balance when she spotted John's Honda parked beside her mom's Jeep. There had been a time when Declan and John shared the Honda, but that was before Gloria's accident. Lately, she'd spotted Declan driving his mom's large golden Mercedes. Once, he had complained that it made him feel like a real estate agent, to which his mom had quipped, "And that's a good thing, right?"

Declan had told Lizbet he didn't think it was a good thing. But Lizbet guessed that since his mom could no longer drive and his own truck was no longer drivable, it made sense for him to tool around in a Mercedes that looked as if it was designed for home buyers and sellers. She wondered if it still bothered him. It bothered her that she didn't know how or what he was feeling.

Lizbet puttered the bike into the barn, parked it, slipped off her helmet, and greeted the horses in their stalls. "Is John here?" she asked Trotter after petting his silky nose.

Trotter nodded and twitched his tail.

"Anyone know why?" Lizbet asked, her gaze traveling from the horses to the goats milling about in their pen. They tended to be more intelligent than the horses, but also more self-centered so less likely to take note of something that didn't involve their own dinners. But all the animals thrived on gossip and Lizbet relied on that.

The horses nickered and the goats bleated, but no one really told her anything.

"So... no one's with him?" she persisted.

"Your mom," Sally the goat told her.

The tension in Lizbet's neck eased as she stroked the animals, complimented them on their good behavior, and wished them all a good night.

An amber-colored moon hovered over the tops of the distant trees. A honey moon. Professor Madison had explained that the term "honeymoon" dates back to the fifth century, when the moon cycles marked time. Back then, a newlywed couple drank mead, a honey-based alcoholic drink believed to have aphrodisiac properties, during their first moon of marriage.

Lizbet watched her mom and John through the kitchen window. Their laughter floated through the glass separating them from Lizbet. Although they both wore aprons and their hands were sticky with dough, John

looked like he'd been sprinkled with flour. It dusted his hair, his jaw, and his clothes.

He said something and Daugherty responded by bumping him with her shoulder. Lizbet couldn't see their faces, but she knew they were smiling. She also knew they belonged together.

And what would that mean for her? Would Declan be a part of family gatherings? Would she have to sit across from his future wife at the Thanksgiving table? Would she watch his children scramble for presents under a Christmas tree? Maybe someday she'd be okay with that thought, but not tonight. She couldn't chit-chat with John and pretend that her heart didn't ache for Declan.

She walked as quietly as she could to the front, padded up the porch, and tried the door. Locked.

She glanced at the giant maple tree beside her grandmother's house. The branches brushed alongside an upstairs bathroom window. Without giving it any more thought, she swung up into the tree. She had only reached the third branch when the call of crows stopped her.

"Death! Death!" they screeched.

Lizbet hugged the tree to keep from falling. "Whose?" she asked.

"Sheep! Sheep!"

Lizbet's thoughts flashed to the few sheep on her grandmother's farm. Chet, fluffy and white, Charleen, dusty black, and tiny Chuckie, the not-quite-white lamb with a black nose.

"Neighboring farm," a crow cawed.

Lizbet blew out a sigh of relief but then felt immediately guilty. She scrambled out of the tree, skinning her arms and legs in her haste. "What happened?" she asked.

But before the birds could answer, Elizabeth banged out the door, followed by John and Daugherty. They all began running for the barn. No one noticed her beneath the tree.

"What happened?" she repeated in a harsh whisper.

But the birds had flown away.

Lizbet took off. She caught up to her grandmother first. "What's going on?" she asked through panted breaths.

"We have to get all of the animals into the barn and batten the hatches," Elizabeth said as she slid a bolt through the barn's double doors.

"I think most of the animals are already in the barn for the night," Lizbet said.

"We have to make sure!" Elizabeth huffed, leaned against the barn, and placed a hand on her heart. "Getting old isn't for softies!"

"Neither is running a ranch," Lizbet said. "Are you okay?" She looped her arm around her grandmother's waist.

"I'm fine! I'm not the one we need to worry about!" Elizabeth said. "I'll go right and you go left."

"John and Mom are already circling the barn," Lizbet said. "Why don't you stay here—"

"I'm not a sissy!" Elizabeth tried to walk, but staggered.

Lizbet guided her to a bench and helped her sit. "Just tell me what happened."

"It was the wolves..." Elizabeth gasped, clutching at her shirt near her heart.

"Where? Here?" Lizbet glanced up at the amber-colored moon hanging in the sky.

"At the Hernandez's." Elizabeth doubled over and put her head between her knees.

"Did you talk to Perez?"

"Matias."

John and her mom jogged around opposite corners of the barn. Her mom reached them first. John had his phone pressed against his ear.

"Come as soon as you can," he said, before returning his phone to his pocket.

Lizbet wanted to ask who he was talking to, but couldn't make herself say the words.

John answered her unspoken question. "Declan's friend, Baxter, has a drone. He's bringing it over. Although we might not be able to see the wolves in the dark."

Lizbet peered into the forest. Something moved in the shadows. She started after it. John placed a warning hand on her arm, stopping her.

"You can't go in there," he said.

"But—"

"He's right," Daugherty said.

"It's much too dangerous," Elizabeth said.

"They won't hurt me."

"I'm sure that's what Declan's grandfather thought, too," Daugherty said.

Lizbet clenched her jaw and dropped onto the bench beside her grandmother. "We have to do something."

"We have. All of our animals are accounted for and locked up in the barn, except for the chickens in their coop," her mom said. "Everyone is safe in their beds. I suggest we do the same." She pulled on Elizabeth's arm. "Come on, Mom. Let's go to bed."

"I can't go to bed!" Elizabeth refused to budge. "How could I sleep knowing my animals are in danger?"

"I can sleep in the barn with the animals," Lizbet said.

Before anyone could shoot her suggestion down, Declan's mom's car pulled down the drive.

"Okay, you." Daugherty pulled on her mother's hand. "Reinforcements have arrived. We women-folk can go to bed."

"Shame on you, Daugherty Westmoor!" Elizabeth shook off her daughter's grip. "I didn't raise you to be such a pantywaist."

Lizbet lost all interest in her grandmother and mom's argument when Declan climbed out of the car. He had a contraption tucked under his arm as he strode their way. Moonlight touched his hair.

"Come on, Grandma," Lizbet pleaded, urgency touching her voice. "There's nothing we can do out here." She was

concerned for her grandmother, of course, but she also didn't think she could be around Declan and pretend her heart wasn't bleeding. She longed to go back to the way they had been before the argument, before the accident, before everything became stilted and strange.

"Grandma, let me make you some tea," Lizbet said as she helped Elizabeth into the house.

"Stop fussing over me like I'm an old lady!" Elizabeth huffed and plopped down on the bench in the mudroom. She fumbled with the ties on her boots.

Lizbet stood, watching, her fingers itching to help, but holding her tongue. After a few indecisive moments, she went into the kitchen, pulled out some mugs, and filled the kettle with water.

A buzzing noise filled the air.

"What's that?" Elizabeth barked.

Lizbet glanced into the mudroom and noticed that Elizabeth had made little headway on her bootlaces. "That must be Baxter's drone."

"Baxter? Baxter who?"

Lizbet tried to tell herself that Elizabeth was angry and frustrated by her own aging body and mind—and not being intentionally cranky and mean. "Baxter is Declan's friend."

"I don't really see what good that thing can do. It's not as if wolves can't move."

She had a point. "What do you think we should do?" Lizbet stood by the stove, waiting for the kettle to sing.

Elizabeth, finally free of her boots, padded into the kitchen in her stocking feet and took a chair at the table. Her gray hair was Einsteinesque. Fatigue etched her wrinkled face.

Her mom would want Elizabeth to go to bed, but Lizbet suspected Elizabeth wouldn't be able to sleep. "Would you like me to make some cookies?"

"What good will that do?" Elizabeth snapped.

"Cookies can never hurt. Cookies are harmless." Lizbet pulled out the flour canister and set it on the counter before selecting the vanilla, cinnamon, and molasses from the cupboard.

"Tell that to a diabetic," Elizabeth grumbled.

Lizbet pressed her lips together, pulled her shoulders back, and got the eggs and butter from the fridge. She wondered when and if Declan would come in and if he'd notice that she was making his favorite cookies.

Daugherty and John pressed through the dark woods while Declan followed. Wind whipped through the trees and the branches moaned in complaint. Clouds hurried through the sky as if they were late for somewhere they had to be—somewhere important.

John and Daugherty both carried guns. Declan did not, because, as his dad had said, Declan didn't know how to use one. Declan suspected that the same could be said of his dad, but he didn't point this out. He would much rather follow the drone and watch the screen on the controller than accidentally shoot his own foot. Or someone else.

He guided the drone slightly above the tree's canopy, searching for movement on the ground. The gray wolves would blend into the night's shadows. The trees dancing in the wind complicated their search. His hopes were low.

He wished Lizbet were with them.

"What's that?" Daugherty's whisper came out as a hiss. She used the rifle as a pointer.

Declan didn't see anything unusual, but his dad must have. He jogged forward and plucked something shiny out of the dirt.

"It's a dog collar," John said, turning it in his hands and reading the tag. "Tickles. Isn't that Baxter's dog?"

Declan nodded. "He got lost in the woods a few weeks ago, but he came home the next morning."

John tossed Declan the collar. Declan caught it and slipped it into his pocket without looking at it.

The woods gave way to a moonlit valley. On the drone controller screen, Declan saw a tall and rangy creature emerge from the woods. He froze, staring.

"What is it?" John asked.

"I'm not sure," Declan said slowly.

His dad and Daugherty came to watch the screen.

"It looks like a giant dog," Declan said, "but definitely not a wolf."

"I've never seen a dog like that," Daugherty whispered.

John took the controller from Declan and tried looking at it from different angles. Above them, the drone dipped and zigzagged. Declan grabbed it back. "Dad! You're going to crash it!" He steadied it.

"Sorry, I thought the drone could be distorting the image."

"We have to see it for ourselves," Daugherty whispered.

John nodded, and crept toward the clearing, his gun raised.

We are made from Mother Earth
and we go back to Mother Earth.
— Shenandoah

Chapter Thirteen

The next morning, before anyone else woke, Lizbet tiptoed into the kitchen and poked through the trash, looking for targets. She gathered a collection of tin cans and empty bottles, placed them in a paper bag, and headed outside. The warm summer air hit Lizbet when she opened the back door. The wind had swept the sky cloud-free, leaving the morning bright and clear. Leaves and branches lay scattered over the yard and driveway and, still wearing pajamas, Lizbet picked her way through the fallen bracken to the barn, where she took care of the animals, filling the feeders and opening the gates.

She murmured to the horses as she weaved between them, their gentle manners and bulk reassuring her. The goats, with their cold noses bumping against her bare thighs, pressed against her in their hurry for freedom. This is real life, she told herself, although she had learned not too long ago that reality could shift dramatically.

After the animals were cared for, Lizbet lined up the cans on the split-rail fence and took forty paces back. The horses nickered a greeting; she felt the curious gazes of the goats. She cocked and shouldered the gun. First the bottles. Watching them explode into silvery dust, she felt only a little better. The cans, even though they didn't shatter, made a satisfactory tinging sound when hit. The horses pranced around the corral, bucking, kicking and complaining about the noise reverberating through the valley.

Today, she determined as she reloaded and cocked the gun, she would find answers.

"Can you teach me how to do that?" a voice said directly behind her.

She started, whirled around, and pointed the gun at Declan's chest.

It took a few seconds for her heart to slow.

Declan grinned, placed his hand on the barrel of the gun, and lowered it.

"Sorry," she said with a slow exhale. "You scared me."

"Same here," he said.

"You want to learn how to shoot?"

He nodded. "I'd ask my dad to teach me, but I'm pretty sure he doesn't know anything more than me, even though he was acting all ballsy for your mom last night."

"My mom said you saw a creature but it wasn't a wolf."

"It did not look like any wolf I've ever seen."

"So, what did it look like?"

He paused. "This will sound crazy. It looked like a giant Tickles."

"Tickles? Baxter's Schnauzer?"

Declan nodded.

"There are Giant Schnauzers. That must have been what you saw."

"It was really giant."

"They're big..." Lizbet reached into her pocket, pulled out some bullets, and reloaded the gun.

"Wait, teach me what you're doing," Declan said.

Lizbet emptied the cartridge and reloaded again, going much slower so he could watch.

"Where did you learn this?"

"From my mom on the island. I'm sure she learned it from Elizabeth."

"But why? You're vegetarian. It's not like you were hunting for food."

Lizbet cocked the gun. "No. It was more about protection. I didn't aim at the foxes, but I would use the gun to scare them away from the henhouse."

"You could have used a rock," Declan pointed out.

She grinned and handed him the gun. "I could have, but I didn't. Do you want to learn or not?"

He took it from her.

"Careful…" She showed him how to hold it. "Always keep the muzzle pointed in a safe direction. It's the first and most important rule in shooting."

She lifted the butt so it was braced into the pocket of his shoulder. "The gun is going to kick back, so you can't have it on your collarbone. It needs to be right here." She lowered the butt of the gun a smidgen. "Otherwise, you'll get hurt." She placed his hands where they needed to be. "This is your trigger hand, but keep your finger off the trigger even when the safety is on. Use your left hand to balance the stock. Now find your steady position."

Declan closed one eye. "Steady position?"

She nodded, placed her hands on his hips and shifted him. "Your hip of the non-trigger hand wants to be pointed like this at your target."

He nodded as if he couldn't feel the energy zipping between them. Lizbet stepped away from him. "I'm going to put the cans back on the fence, so don't shoot me." She took her time locating the tin cans. They were scattered throughout the pasture's tall grass. She felt his gaze on her, but she didn't hurry. Standing so close to him had sent her blood racing. She needed a moment. He was like a drug, and she the junkie. She had to be okay around him. If things worked out between their parents, as she hoped they would, she had to be able to be a sane person around him.

She waded through the tall grass. The early morning dew soaked the hems of her pajama bottoms. She slid

a quick glance at Declan in his jeans and white T-shirt. His hair was mussed, but at least he was dressed—which was more than she could say. It occurred to her that she probably looked ridiculous in her pink hoodie, floral PJ bottoms, and boots. She hadn't even run a comb through her curls or brushed her teeth. Feeling fuddled, she picked up one dented can after another, hoping that by the time she finished, her sanity would return. She lined the tin cans up on the rail.

"You said you saw the wolves," Declan said.

"Wolf," she corrected him. "I saw one wolf."

"And it didn't look like a Giant Schnauzer."

"No, it was definitely a wolf." She reached his side. "Are you ready to try?"

He nodded.

"Contrary to what you've heard, you're not going to pull the trigger. You press it. Ready?"

Declan bit his lip, took aim, and rested his finger on the trigger for a half-second before pressing down.

BOOM.

Some distant branch in the woods cracked.

He lowered the gun, his expression sheepish. "I guess I missed."

"It feels really good to be better at something than you," Lizbet told him.

He shouldered the gun. "Don't get used to it," he said with a grin and took aim at the cans. He fired and another distant branch snapped. "I'm hurting innocent trees."

"Yes..." A thought occurred to her. "The night Tickles disappeared, it was what? Three or four weeks ago?"

"About that. Why?"

"And there was a full moon."

An emotion Lizbet couldn't read flickered across Declan's face. She thought it might be disappointment. He already thought she was strange. If he knew what she was thinking, he would probably be more than disappointed. He'd also be disgusted. She brushed her hands on her PJs and watched Declan take aim and shoot.

Boom! Ting! A can flew off the fence.

"You hit one!"

He beamed at her, triumphant.

"Hey, I gotta go," she told him.

"Why?"

"There's someone I gotta see."

"Oh, of course." He tried to hide his disappointment.

"You can just bring the gun inside when you're done practicing," she told him over her shoulder before she turned to run to the house.

In her room, Lizbet threw on some clothes while her mind raced. She needed advice, but she wasn't sure who to turn to.

Back home, Declan found his mom holding a tea party with Leo Cabriolet in the dining room. He had only ever seen the attorney in business clothes, so he was surprised to find him in tennis whites. It was like the time he'd come across a picture of LeBron James playing a violin. It jarred him, but didn't totally surprise him.

A platter of cookies and a pot of tea sat on the table between them. A quick glance at his mom's clean, crumb-free plate told him she hadn't tried to feed herself in front of Cabriolet. This also didn't surprise him.

He slammed the door to alert them of his presence. They both started, as if guilty.

Cabriolet jumped to his feet. "Declan, I'm glad you're here." He tossed his napkin onto the table.

Declan raised an eyebrow. He hated his stepfather, but he also hated that his mom seemed to be already on the prowl just weeks after Godwin's disappearance. Especially since he felt that all her attention should be focused on healing and learning how to be left-handed. Declan didn't think there was any room on her to-do list for schmoozing the lawyer.

"There's been an incident at the winery," Cabriolet said.

"What sort of incident?" If the attorney had told him the winery had been overrun by Giant Schnauzers, Declan wouldn't have been surprised.

"The manager, Mr. Eldridge, had a heart attack," Gloria replied.

"That's terrible," Declan said, stepping into the room.

"If we had sold the winery as I suggested weeks ago—" his mom began.

"I'm sure he would have still had a heart attack," Declan said. "It's not like the winery caused his heart disease."

"Of course not," Cabriolet murmured.

"But his condition wouldn't be our problem," Gloria said.

"Should we send flowers? Is he home?" Declan asked.

"He died," Cabriolet told him.

"Oh." Declan took a seat at the table, trying to process everything that this news could mean for him and the winery. "Well, of course we'll send flowers and a card. He has a family?"

Frustration flashed across Gloria's face. "His family isn't our concern—"

"No? How do you figure?" Declan asked.

"The problem is," Cabriolet said, "Mr. Eldridge was the only one who knew the recipe."

"What?" Declan rocked back in his chair. "That's insane!"

Cabriolet nodded. "You're right. It is."

Declan's mind flashed to something Lizbet had told him. "Wait, I know someone with a recipe... They claimed it was much better than Igasho." He snagged a cookie off the table and bounced to his feet.

"Where are you going?" Gloria asked.

"I have an idea," he said.

The doorbell rang.

Declan hurried across the room and threw open the door. Holbrook St. James stood on the porch, backlit by the early afternoon sun. "Hey! You're probably not the person to ask, but could you arrange for a bouquet and card to be sent to Mr. Eldridge's family?"

If the accountant was surprised, he didn't show it. He simply nodded as Declan pushed past him toward the garage and the Mercedes. It wasn't until Declan was driving away that he paused to wonder what St. James was doing at his mom's house dressed in jeans and a pullover sweater.

As he thought of seeing Lizbet again, Declan's blood raced. Spending the morning with her, standing so close to her, the gentle touch of her hands on his, the memories made him dizzy. Even as she'd bolted, his mind had jumped from one excuse to see her again to another. He told himself he had to get a grip, but he also wondered why. Yeah, he'd been mad that she wouldn't tell him how she knew there would be an accident, that she claimed to have some voodoo powers that gave her glimpses of the future that were spookily accurate. Of course he didn't believe in any of that. But he believed in her. He absolutely believed she had the power to send his pulse into hyper-drive. Was that enough?

He paused beside the car. The still-warm engine radiated heat through the garage. Forty minutes ago he'd been at Lizbet's grandmother's ranch and now, not even an hour later, he'd come up with another excuse to see her again. He rubbed his chin, feeling pathetic and like a stalker.

His memory tripped back to the conversation. She'd had the wine at Matias's grandmother's house. Wouldn't it make more sense to go to the Hernandez's? He made up his mind and climbed into the car. Gripping the steering wheel, he told himself that his main concern was the wine. Not Lizbet. He turned the ignition. Of course, the Hernandez farm was right next door to Elizabeth's ranch. If he was lucky, he'd bump into Lizbet.

He drove the miles in tight-lipped silence. It wasn't easy to drive past Elizabeth's ranch without turning down the driveway, but he did it. To his surprise, he found Baxter's Jeep parked in front of the Hernandez's' farmhouse. Of course, he knew that Baxter and Maria had gone out a few times, but he wasn't sure if having Baxter around made his mission easier or more difficult. He climbed from the car and called out to Baxter and Maria who were seated at the patio table engaged in a watermelon seed spitting contest.

The news that Lizbet and Matias were together hit him like a punch to the face. His shock must have registered, because Maria added, "I can take you there, if you wish."

"What about pickle ball?" Baxter asked, looking put out.

Maria laughed and placed her hand on his chest. "My grandmother's wine is way better than a pickle ball game."

"How do you know?" Baxter asked. "You've never played pickle ball."

She tapped his chest with one finger. "And you have obviously never had my grandmother's wine. If you had, you would agree with me."

"We can fix that," Declan said in a sullen voice. Why would Lizbet go with Matias to his grandmother's house? And this wasn't the first time, a jealous voice in his head whispered. A more reasonable voice reminded him that their breakup had been his idea. He shut down the voices in his head.

"Doesn't your mom have the recipe?" Declan asked.

"She does, but she'd never give it to you," Maria told him. "She's scared of Mawmaw. Everyone is."

"Why?" Baxter asked.

"Because that's the proper response. You should be scared of her." Maria held up her finger. "Wait here, I'll be right back." She put down her half-eaten watermelon slice, wiped her hands on a napkin, and headed for the kitchen.

Declan and Baxter looked at each other, both with questions in their eyes that Declan didn't want to ask or answer. Instead, he pulled the dog collar out of his jeans pocket. "I found this last night."

Baxter turned the collar over in his hands. "So weird."

"Why? We know he got lost a few weeks ago."

"And last night," Baxter added.

"Really?"

"Yeah. We couldn't find him and ended up leaving the back door open and going to bed. This morning, we found him. Just like last time, he had blood all over him, but after a bath, it would appear that none of it was his. No wounds."

"That happened last time? You didn't tell me that."

"I thought I did."

Maria claimed all of Baxter's attention by just walking out the door. She jingled her keys at them. "Guys. I can't wait for you to try my grandmother's wine."

"Why?"

"It has... well, you'll see." She headed for a beat-up pickup as if she knew they'd follow without question. That was what they did.

Because Declan was expecting a giant, scary old woman, the tiny, wizened woman sitting on the porch surprised him. Lizbet was sitting beside her, looking entranced. Matias lounged at her feet. Their conversation came to a stop as soon as Maria pulled the truck down the driveway.

Jealousy began its rant in Declan's mind. He tried to hush it, to tamp it down, but it wouldn't be still. Why was she with Matias? Had she kissed him? How could she go from her morning with Declan to an afternoon with Matias? And she'd practically run away from Declan. Why?

Insecurity reared its ugly head. Did she prefer Matias's company? Could he make her laugh? Had she been thinking about Matias when she was with Declan?

Baxter nudged him, making Declan realize he needed to open the door of the truck.

Irritation zipped through Lizbet as soon as she saw Maria's pickup pull down the driveway. She still had questions and they weren't the sort of questions just anyone would understand, let alone answer. Her frustration gave way to shock when she spotted Declan and Baxter squished into the pickup's tiny cab. Baxter alone could fill a pickup's cab. Declan was one basketball player too many.

She definitely couldn't ask Mawmaw questions in front of Declan. She didn't stop to wonder why she felt comfortable talking about werewolves in front of Matias but not Declan. She already knew why.

But then as an idea struck her, she realized that Baxter and Declan's appearance at Matias's grandmother's was a blessing and not the curse she'd originally thought. She elbowed Matias. "We need to go," she said.

He glanced over his shoulder at the approaching truck. Surprise and a certain amount of smugness flashed across his expression. He probably thought she wanted to leave because of Declan—and she did—but it was more than that. It was more about Baxter than Declan, because if Baxter was here, that meant he wasn't at his house and Tickles would be alone.

"But our talk has just begun," Mawmaw said.

"I'm sorry, Mawmaw," Lizbet said. "But this isn't a conversation I wish to have in front of Maria's friends."

Mawmaw cocked her head, considering Lizbet. "Is this because of who they are, or rather, who you are?"

Lizbet pushed to her feet and replied, "Probably a combination of both."

Mawmaw smiled. "Wise answer." Grabbing the arms of her rocking chair, she slowly pushed herself to a standing position. "Let me get the things you'll need."

A few weeks ago, Declan had thought he could read Lizbet, but now he realized how wrong he'd been. And if he'd been wrong then, was it possible he was wrong now? And had been all along?

He had been so into her. Still was, if he was honest with himself. He had assumed she'd felt the same. So why was she so anxious to leave? Moments ago, before she'd noticed him, she'd seemed engrossed in whatever Matias's grandmother was saying, but as soon as she saw him, she was like a deer twitching in headlights—ready to bolt.

With Matias Hernandez.

Part of Declan blamed himself. He was the one who had first pulled away from their relationship. What had he thought would happen? That Lizbet would just stay at the ranch, waiting for him?

"It's really great snuggling up with you in this truck cab made for two," Baxter said, "but if you don't open the

door soon and set me free, I'm going to have to assume that you want to make out and then I'll have to punch you."

Declan wrenched open the door and climbed out. Once Baxter was out, Declan shoved him from behind. "Don't be such a homophobe."

"I'm going to let that go," Baxter said.

"Guys!" Maria hushed them. "You have to be super respectful of my grandparents."

"And your brother?"

Maria nodded. "He might be smaller than you, but he can be mean."

Little dog complex, Declan thought. But to be fair, Matias had the build of an athlete and no one would ever call him a dog.

Declan felt sick when Lizbet and Matias walked past.

"Are we chasing you away?" Maria asked.

"Not at all." Matias spoke to his sister, but his gaze never left Declan's face. "Lizbet needs to go."

"How come?" Baxter asked.

Matias shifted his glare from Declan to Baxter. "She doesn't need to clear her schedule with you."

Baxter held up his hands. "Yeah, man, I'm just making idle conversation."

"Maria! Darling!" Mawmaw clapped her hands. "What brings you here?"

Declan shot Lizbet a quick look, but she wouldn't meet his gaze. He straightened his spine, walked past Lizbet without another glance and followed Maria up the steps of her grandmother's front porch.

"Hello, Mawmaw." Maria kissed her grandmother's cheek. "I want you to meet my friends, Declan and Baxter."

While Maria explained why they'd come, Declan's attention wandered back to Matias and Lizbet as they walked across the yard, put helmets on, and climbed onto a motorcycle. He wanted to tell her that motorcycles weren't safe and she should ride home with him in Maria's pickup. Sure, it would be tight, but she could sit on his lap.

When Baxter nudged him, he realized he'd missed part of the conversation.

"Tell her about the winery," Baxter said under his breath.

The winery, right.

While Maria took a seat in a rocker beside her grandmother and Baxter leaned back against the porch railing, Declan remained standing, only half aware of what he was saying because ninety-eight percent of his attention was following Matias and Lizbet. Only after they'd roared away on the back of Matias's motorcycle, Lizbet holding onto Matias with both hands, could Declan be fully in the conversation.

"You seem awfully young to be the head of a winery." Maria's grandmother squinted at him.

"My grandfather owned the business. When he passed he left me..." The blank expressions on the others' faces told him that Maria had already explained this. He started

over. "Mr. Eldridge, the manager, recently died, taking with him the only recipe. Maria told me you also had a recipe for blackberry wine. She was, in fact, bragging about it."

Mawmaw's lips tilted into a smile. "And so she should. You probably didn't know that I knew your Mr. Eldridge, a terrible little toad of a man. It is, of course, sad he died at such a young age, but I doubt very many will mourn him."

Declan rocked back on his heels, surprised at her open hostility.

"Eldridge was a tribe member but many considered him a traitor when he went to work for Igasho winery."

"Why?" Declan asked. "Being the manager of a winery is honest work."

"Ah, but you do not understand." Humor glinted in her eyes, and she lifted up both of her pointer fingers. "I must show you." She waved at the empty chairs on the porch. "Please make yourselves at home. I'll be right back."

"Where's she going?" Baxter whispered after Mawmaw headed into the house.

"If you're lucky, to get some wine," Maria whispered back.

"I don't think this is going very well," Declan said under his breath. He took a seat in a rocker and tapped his toes.

"You won't say that after you try the wine," Maria said.

"What do you mean?" Declan asked.

"Just wait until you taste it," Maria said.

Mawmaw pushed through the door, carrying a tray laden with a croft of wine and three goblets. She smiled, exposing her crooked, yellowing teeth, but the glint in her eye wasn't friendly. In her gaze, Declan read a challenge. He took the offered cup.

The one who tells the
stories rules the world.
– Hopi

Chapter Fourteen

Silence has its own music. Amplify it and a void appears, sucking in all the sounds that should have been: chattering squirrels, calling birds, the buzz of insects. Still. Dark. Silence as heavy as water.

Hunger burns the back of my throat and tightens my gut. I pad across the forest floor. A carpeting of pine needles and soft soil muffles my footfalls. Above the trees' canopy, a smattering of stars glisten, pale against a cloud-filled night. Mist shrouds the moon, but even so, I know it's full—full to the point of overflowing.

I see things differently in this strange dark forest. My perspective shifts as her touch brushes my shoulder. Her scent fills my head. Fear prickles the back of my neck. But I do not fear for myself. Not exactly. I worry for her. For me. I fear my hungry passion will destroy us both.

*D*eclan slammed the goblet back onto the tray as his vision cleared. "What the hell was that?"

Maria beamed at him. "It worked for you, didn't it? What did you see?"

Declan touched his forehead as if checking for a fever.

"What?" Baxter looked confused. He took a long drink of his wine.

Declan waited for his expression to gloss over the way he was sure his had, but Baxter's amiable features didn't shift or change. Declan turned to Maria. "What is that?" he repeated. "It's alcoholic?"

Mawmaw shook her head.

"Some sort of hallucinogen?"

Again Mawmaw shook her head.

Baxter frowned at his drink. "Obviously, I've been ripped off."

"It's wild," Maria said.

"The wine at Igasho..." Declan began.

"Is a sad imitation," Mawmaw finished.

"I want that," Declan said, nodding at the croft.

"Do you really?" Mawmaw murmured. "Ask yourself, is this wise?"

"What is it?" Declan blinked. "Some sort of drug?"

"You're asking if it's illegal. No."

"Why didn't it work for me?" Baxter asked again.

"It's selective," Mawmaw told Declan.

"Obviously," Declan murmured. "So it worked for me, but not Baxter?"

"This time," Maria said. "Next time it might work for Baxter and not you."

Declan itched to try it again, but he didn't dare. He was afraid of getting drunk or high and losing his ability to negotiate. "This wine—"

"Is not for sale," Mawmaw said.

"But—"

She held up a hand to stop him. "Do not ask again."

"What did you see?" Maria repeated.

"I was in the woods. It was dark, but the moon was full."

"Nothing happened?" Maria asked.

He shrugged, considering whether to tell them about the girl who'd been beside him. Had it been Lizbet? He had assumed so, but he couldn't be sure. "There was someone there."

"And?" Maria pressed.

"The vision wasn't very long," Declan told her.

"It's nice to have something more to go on—something concrete to remember," Maria said. "Oh well, it doesn't always come true."

Baxter sat up. "Are you telling me that the wine can make you see into the future?"

"Not always," Mawmaw said.

Not ever, Declan thought. But then, he wasn't so sure.

"It tells you what you need to know."

"So I guess it thinks I don't need to know anything?" Baxter twirled his glass and frowned at the frothing bubbles.

Maria nudged him with her foot. "Maybe you already know everything."

"Well, of course that's what I thought, but I didn't want to say," Baxter joked, but his expression read disappointment.

Matias slowed the motorcycle as they approached Baxter Dresden's property. He used his feet to roll the bike past the wide stretch of lawn. The windows looked blank and dark and the driveway was empty. Of course, cars could be in the garage and people could be inside the house. But Lizbet wasn't interested in people.

"Are you sure about this?" Matias asked.

"No! But it's worth a try, right?"

Lizbet could only see the back of Matias's helmet, so she could only guess he was rolling his eyes. "She's your grandmother!"

"But—werewolves?" He twisted to gaze at her.

"Technically, this would be a were-Schnauzer."

"It's craziness."

Lizbet nodded. "Yep."

"But you still want to do it?"

"How many sheep did you lose?"

Matias's face paled. "Five."

She touched his hand. "I'm sorry."

He closed his eyes for a long moment. "Yeah, me too."

"According to the Internet, the full moon only lasts for three days, and since last night was the first one, we only have today and tomorrow."

"We could just wait..."

"And risk losing more sheep?"

Matias shook his head. "But dognapping...?"

"We won't be dognapping. That can only happen if the dog doesn't want to come." She paused, trying to think of the right words without actually telling him of her ability. "Tickles won't mind. He likes me."

"He's a Schnauzer. He probably likes everyone."

"All we have to do is have the ritual prepped and spend the night with him. If he turns, then we preform the ritual."

"As I said, craziness."

"Will you help me or not?"

Matias cast a worried glance at the house. "Do you think there's an alarm system?"

"Probably. Let's look for a sign. You go around the front and I'll go to the back."

Matias huffed, twisted his lips, and looked as if he wanted to argue.

She touched his hand. "Your family can't lose any more sheep."

He dipped his head in agreement or defeat—she wasn't sure which. They climbed off the bike, and Matias rolled it out of sight behind the boughs of a cedar tree.

⚜

Lizbet waited for Matias to jog around to the front of the property before running to the back. She scanned the yard. A bunny nibbled on the grass near the woods. A chipmunk scampered up a maple tree. Lizbet let out a soft, high whistle.

Tickles poked his head out from under the bench where he'd been resting.

Lizbet patted her leg. "Come here," she urged.

"I can't," he whimpered. *"Electric invisible fence."*

"Can you meet me behind the shed?"

He nodded.

Lizbet glanced around before darting out of the woods and taking shelter behind a storage shed. Tickles wiggled his whole body by way of a greeting.

"Lizbet?" Matias called from the other side of the house.

"Quick," Lizbet whispered as she dropped to squat in front of the dog, "tell me where you were last night."

"Why?"

She petted his ears and ruffled his fur. "You would never hurt anyone, right?"

"Bad guys." The Schnauzer rolled onto his back so she could rub his belly. *"Hurting bad guys is my job."*

Lizbet scratched his belly until he moaned with pleasure. "But have you ever actually done that?" she asked.

"I didn't say I was good at my job." He kicked all four legs in the air and squirmed.

She paused. "No one would call a sheep a bad guy."

Tickles froze. *"What are you implying?"*

"Lizbet?" Matias called again, sounding closer.

"You don't want to hurt anyone, do you?" Lizbet whispered. "You're a good dog."

Tickles whimpered and rolled onto his belly. *"I've been having these nightmares."*

She stroked the top of his head. "Come and stay with me tonight. I want to try and stop your nightmares."

The dog whined. *"I can't. I can't leave. The fence will shock me."*

"Is it new?"

Tickles nodded. *"My masters just put it up this morning. It hurts if I try to leave! It feels like my fur is going catch on fire."*

"If you promise not to run away, I can keep the fence from hurting you."

"Lizbet?" Matias rounded the corner and released a sigh. "Didn't you hear me?"

"Look who I found." Lizbet sat in the dirt and pulled Tickles onto her lap so she could remove his brand new electronic collar.

"I don't feel good about this," Matias said.

"We'll be fine," Lizbet said as she tossed Tickles' collar into a fern. It crackled and sparked as they walked away.

They tramped through the woods until they reached a tree with ascending pieces of wood hammered into its trunk.

Matias gazed upward. "What's this?"

"My mom and her dad built a treehouse when she was a little girl."

"Is it safe?"

"Sure. She brought me here shortly after she regained consciousness and tried to tell me all about her life before the island." Lizbet gazed up at the wooden structure about fifteen feet above the ground. It seemed like the perfect place for what they needed to do.

"And how are we going to get the dog up there?" Matias asked.

"Yes, that's the tricky part, but I do have a plan."

"I'm glad you have a plan, but... that's the tricky part? How about when we're trapped in a tiny space with a werewolf?"

"I thought you didn't believe in werewolves."

"I don't, but still it doesn't hurt to be open minded." He paused. "Unless you're bitten by a were-Schnauzer. I bet that would hurt."

"We aren't going to stay with him." She pointed at a neighboring fir tree. "We're going to watch from there."

"This is nuts!" Matias said.

"I know." Lizbet sighed and folded her arms across her chest. "But it's worth a shot, right?"

Matias made a noise that sounded a lot like a snort.

"How do we get him up there?" he repeated.

"You can carry him in a backpack, but I have to get it and the other things."

"Other things?"

"You know, for the ritual."

"Ritual... right..."

She patted his arm. "You stay here with Tickles and I'll be right back."

"What if he turns into a werewolf... I mean were-Schnauzer while you're gone?"

Lizbet glanced up at the darkening sky. "We have time. I'll be fast." She turned and sprinted through the woods before Matias could argue with her.

She found the old backpack in the garage along with a host of her late grandfather's camping supplies. With Elizabeth snoozing in her easy chair in front of the TV and Daugherty at John's trying out new recipes in the kitchen, Lizbet was confident she wouldn't be interrupted as she borrowed a pair of leather gardening gloves from the potting shed, a hammer from the workbench, a sprig of sage in the garden, a pound of raw hamburger from the fridge, and a silver spoon from the dining room sideboard. After stuffing all her stash into the backpack, she hurried out into the yard.

She froze when Declan's mom's Mercedes turned down the drive.

RUN! a voice in her head screamed. But it was too late, he'd already seen her. She had to get rid of him, but how could she do that without further alienating him? Glancing up at the sinking sun, she prayed it could give her answers. It glowed warm and pink and silent.

Declan cut the engine and climbed from the car. "Hey," he said softly, "I want to talk. Is this a good time?"

"No, not really." She tried to think of excuses that wouldn't sound crazy... *I have to go before the full moon rises and Tickles turns into a were-Schnauzer. Or, I'd love to chat, but if I don't hurry and administer the curse ritual more sheep will die. Or...*

"Are you going camping?" He pointed at the backpack in her hand.

"Yes!" It was not quite a lie.

"By yourself?"

"No..." If she told him she was going with Matias, how would he feel? Maybe he wouldn't care. That thought hurt. And she didn't want to hurt him, in case he did care, because looking at him in the fading purple twilight, she knew that she cared about him. A lot. On impulse, she dropped the backpack and wrapped her arms around him. "I hate that things are so weird between us."

"Me too," he said in a strangled voice.

She pulled away from him. "Can we talk tomorrow? There's someone waiting for me right now."

He gazed over the pasture. The Hernandez's' farm lay on the other side of the forest. His lips tightened and his shoulders slumped. "Okay, tomorrow. What time?"

"I don't know... You pick."

"Noon. We'll go to lunch. Does that work?"

"Sure. As friends?"

"Sure. Friends."

"'K, see you." She turned and ran without looking back. Even though she really, really wanted to.

Back at the treehouse, Lizbet emptied the backpack to make room for Tickles. When the collection lay at her feet, Matias held open the backpack while Lizbet attempted to wrestle the dog inside.

Tickles kicked and whined. *"It smells of fish and bacon,"* he complained. *"And I was just groomed last week!"*

"You like fish and bacon," Lizbet said through clenched teeth.

Tickles yipped. *"But I don't want to smell like them! I could end up chewing my own fur!"*

"Get in!" Lizbet growled. "You don't want to be a were-Schnauzer, right?"

"Wow, it's like you two are actually talking to each other," Matias said.

Lizbet straightened and gave him a dirty look. "Don't be ridiculous."

"I'm being ridiculous? You're the one who thinks we can tame a were-Schnauzer!"

Tickles sniffed and relaxed into the backpack. Lizbet tightened the strings so he couldn't climb out before she hefted it up and held it out so Matias could put it on.

"Schnauzers, everybody's wearing them this season," she said, adjusting the straps on Matias's shoulders.

"Ready?" he asked.

"As I'll ever be," she said.

Matias tugged at the wooden slats hammered into the tree. "I'm not sure these will hold me. You better wait until I'm up to follow. I don't want to fall and take you down with me."

"I don't like this," Tickles whimpered.

"Stop being such a puppy," Lizbet grumbled.

Fading light flickered through the wooden slats of the treehouse. Lizbet set the hamburger package on the floor, pulled open the plastic, crumbled up the sage and sprinkled it on top, filling the air with its sweet, tangy scent.

The treehouse had three walls, a roof and a floor all made of scrap lumber. Tiny Lizbet could stand upright, but Matias had to stoop. It was tight quarters.

She handed the spoon and hammer to Matias. "Here, you'll be better at this than me."

He took them and quirked an eyebrow.

"We need silver dust."

"You expect me to pulverize this?"

She patted his shoulder. "You can do it."

"This will be easier against a rock," he groused. "You should have told me to do this before I climbed up here."

She gave him an apologetic smile.

As soon as he hit the ground, Lizbet squatted beside Tickles and began petting him.

Within minutes, she heard the ringing sound of a hammer on stone.

"Now remember," she said to Tickles with a warning in her voice, "do not eat this unless you're a werewolf." She nodded at the hamburger mixture.

"Why? Is it poisonous?"

"Possibly. But according to the Internet it cures wolfism. It shouldn't kill you, but I wouldn't try it."

"But I can't remember anything about being a wolf. Those nights are a total blank. I'm not sure I have any control…"

Lizbet stroked his head. "It must be terrifying."

Tickles waggled his head.

"You're a good dog," she murmured.

The hammering stopped. Lizbet looked over the edge of the treehouse floor. Matias climbed hand over hand, one fist curled. "How much of this do you need?"

"Not a ton," she said. "Where is it?"

Matias opened his fist and dumped a smattering of silvery bits into the pile of hamburger.

Lizbet scooted next to it, and began to mix it with her bare hands.

"That is disgusting," Matias said, kneeling beside her. "All that meat—not to mention the silver—can't be good for the dog."

"But if it can save your dad's sheep, it's worth it, right?"

"Right." His shoulder brushed hers. "But in my mind, there's like a ninety-nine percent chance that the dog remains a dog and a hundred percent chance that the dog wolfs that down as soon as we turn our backs."

"He won't do that," Lizbet said.

"You sound so sure."

"Look, he's not even interested in it now." She pushed the meat concoction to the back corner of the treehouse and told Tickles to sit and stay in the opposite corner.

He obeyed, staring at her with his sweet big brown eyes.

"It's like he understands you," Matias murmured.

"Of course he understands me."

"Look." Matias pointed at the moon rising in the east. "I wonder if we have to wait for midnight."

"Come on." She tugged on his arm. "Let's go."

He did his eyebrow thing again.

She laughed at him. "Just to be safe."

He smirked and followed her down the makeshift ladder.

"Be safe, Tickles!" Lizbet called.

"Where to now?" Matias asked.

Lizbet picked up a large maple leaf and used it to wipe off her hands. It helped, but they still felt sticky and gross from the fatty hamburger. She nodded at a neighboring tree.

"Ladies first." Matias swept an arm in front of her.

Lizbet grabbed the closest branch and swung into the tree.

"Can I share your tree, or should I get my own?" Matias asked from the ground.

"How can you make jokes at a time like this? Any second that poor little dog could transform into a monster!"

"Hey! I'm just looking out for your reputation." He put his hands on his hips. "This is the first time I've ever stayed the night with a girl in a tree, and I want to do it right."

She laughed. "Okay, I get that. Thanks for asking. I'll share my tree." She climbed up two more branches.

"Does that mean?" He waggled his eyebrows as he followed her.

"It means if you try anything I'm pushing you off." She gripped a branch above her head while standing on another. "We're here to watch the dog."

"Sounds boring." He paused on a branch two below hers.

His face was even with her belly button. It felt odd to be so much taller than him. "You'll probably wish for a little boredom—"

A howl interrupted her.

"Oh, my," Lizbet breathed, watching Tickles shiver in the moonlight. He grew until he burst through the treehouse's wooden roof. Shards of wood flew through the air. Muscles rippled beneath his glossy coat, his eyes glowed, and his teeth, long and vicious, glistened. He was terrifyingly beautiful.

"No frickin' way," Matias said. His foot slipped and he nearly fell.

Tickles howled again.

"The meat!" Lizbet cried. "Tickles, eat the meat!"

He gazed at her with blazing eyes before shifting his attention to the pile of hamburger in the corner. He wolfed it down in a single bite. His long red tongue licked his chops. He panted, stared at them, and then lunged.

Matias scrambled up the tree as the transformed Tickles flew at them. Lizbet, stunned, lost her grip and fell.

Blackness engulfed her.

Cherish youth but
trust old age.
– Pueblo

Chapter Fifteen

"I didn't know what else to do," Matias said.

"You were right to bring her here," Mawmaw said, peering into Lizbet's face. "How are you feeling, child?"

Lizbet huddled into the sofa and held the icepack against her aching head. "I'll be okay," she said, although she seriously doubted it.

"What happened?" Mawmaw asked.

"You will never believe me," Matias said. "I saw it with my own eyes and I can still hardly believe it." He told her about Tickles' transformation and eventual disappearance.

"Did you warn your father to protect the sheep?"

Matias slapped his forehead. "Of course! I have to do that! I was so worried about you, I couldn't think straight."

"Tell your father now," Mawmaw said.

Matias dug his phone from his pocket and went to stand on the front porch to make the call.

Mawmaw leaned toward Lizbet and lowered her voice. "I'm going to tell you a secret. It's a very powerful secret. If you want to catch your werewolf—really, if you want to do anything—you must see it. But first, you must ask yourself how this is to be done and then you sleep. In your dreams, the answers will come. After they do, you must give thanks to the Great Spirit who sent them, and follow the instructions you receive with pure intention and perfect obedience—even if the answer doesn't make sense. Most people cannot do this. They lack the faith to press forward, but that is how it is done. You must step into the night believing in the answers that will come."

Matias came back into the room and pocketed his phone.

Lizbet wondered what he had told his dad.

Mawmaw stood. "Let me get you something to drink. It will help you sleep." She winked at Lizbet. "Ready, child?"

The next day at noon, Declan stood on Elizabeth's front porch, his hands shoved into his pockets.

"She's not here," Daugherty told him. "She spent the night at Maria's grandmother's house."

Declan swallowed a groan.

"I know what you're thinking," Daugherty said, "but Maria called me. She said Lizbet wasn't feeling well." She cocked her head, considering him. "Their family is terribly old-fashioned. I know there wouldn't be any hanky-panky at their grandparents' house."

Declan thought about the backpack and wondered if Daugherty was certain that Lizbet had stayed at the grandmother's. Or had she been camping in the woods? He pushed his hand through his hair. Yesterday she'd said they should be friends. Maybe he needed to accept that. He started to turn away.

"Huh, Declan?"

He turned back, but kept his eyes averted so Daugherty couldn't see his unshed tears.

"Don't give up on her," Daugherty said. "She's had a strange life and it's all my fault."

He nodded and made his way back to the Mercedes. Inside the car and out of sight from the house, he slammed his palms against the steering wheel and cried.

When Lizbet woke, the sun hung at the top of the sky. She bolted from the sofa, knocking the quilt to the floor and startling the gray-eyed cat lying near where her feet had been seconds ago.

"What time is it?" she demanded.

The cat stretched his paws in front of him and uncurled from the sofa. *"Afternoon, I believe,"* he said.

"Augh!" Lizbet groaned and ran to the front window. Matias's bike still leaned against the fencing surrounding the yard. "I have to get home! Where's Matias?"

"How would I know?" the cat asked. He twirled three times before sinking back onto the sofa and nestling his head onto his paws.

"Ah, there you are." Mawmaw walked into the room carrying a tray laden with breakfast rolls, grapes, and a croft of wine. "I've been waiting for you. Hungry?"

Her stomach growled in response.

Mawmaw chuckled. "There's my answer."

"But I don't have time. I need to get home. I'm meeting someone at noon."

Mawmaw raised her eyebrow and placed the tray on the coffee table. "Noon has come and gone."

Lizbet sank back onto the sofa and wrung her hands. "I need to go," she said in a half-whisper.

"Did you find your answers in your dreams?" Mawmaw poured herself a glass of wine and settled into the chair in front of Lizbet.

"I did..."

"And now you know what you need to do."

Lizbet nodded. She didn't know if her plan could work—mostly because it wasn't all up to her. She couldn't do it alone. She'd need help. Lots of help. And she'd have to

have everything in place before tonight—the last night of August's full moon, or otherwise she'd have to wait for September. It was possible the wolves wouldn't hang around that long. In a month's time, they could easily move on and terrorize farms in other communities. She needed to act now. She bounced back to her feet. "Could you find Matias and tell him I need to get home? I really appreciate all of your wisdom and advice, but now that I know what to do, I need to make it happen."

Mawmaw stood, wrapped her arms around Lizbet, and drew her in for a brief, tight hug. After she'd pulled away, Mawmaw fished inside her apron pocket, pulled out something and pressed it into Lizbet's hand.

The cold and shiny silver bullet glistened in the sunlight streaming through the window. Mawmaw curled her fingers around Lizbet's open palm.

As soon as Matias dropped her off at the ranch, Lizbet bolted across the lawn, but she stopped short when she spotted Tickles sitting on the front porch. Memories of the previous night flashed through her mind and her head began to ache again. She shuffled her feet, no longer sure what to say or do.

"Tickles," she said. "What are you doing here?"

"I've come to thank you," he said.

"For what?"

"For curing me, of course."

"But...you're not cured. I hate to have to tell you this, but I saw you change last night."

He dipped his head in acknowledgement. *"I probably did, but it couldn't have lasted very long. All the other nights I have no memories of the entire night. Last night... well, I was myself hours before the sun came up."* He met her gaze. *"It was a very long night."*

"But Matias said they lost two more sheep."

Tickles rubbed his eyes with his paw. *"It wasn't me."*

She wasn't quite sure whether to believe him, but relief swept through her. She'd been mentally trying to prepare herself to shoot the dog, but she hadn't been quite sure if she'd be able to go through with it. She ruffled the fur between his ears. "Good. I'm glad it's not you." She squatted before him. "Would you like to help me capture a wolf?"

He nodded.

"Good. I want you to tell all the animals to meet me in the back pasture at eight p.m. This has to be a concerted effort."

After dinner, Lizbet set about filling the backpack with the rifle, a tarp, and the pair of night-vision goggles she'd picked up at the sporting goods store. Once she'd doused herself and her clothes in baking soda, she picked up her things and headed for the pasture.

Declan spent the day telling himself that Lizbet wasn't right for him. They were too different. She was too quirky. He didn't have time for a girlfriend. Four years for undergrad, four years for medical school, four years of residency... that was twelve years. He had twelve years to find a normal girlfriend.

But he didn't want a normal girlfriend.

He wanted Lizbet.

Gloria sat at the kitchen table. Not only had she lost weight since the accident—she joked about not being able to feed herself—but she wore her hair and makeup differently. She looked younger, healthier, and surprisingly happier in spite of her useless hand resting in a sling. She looked up from her crossword puzzle as he grabbed the keys off the hook on the wall. "Where you going?"

He swallowed, not knowing if he wanted his mom to stop him or not. "Lizbet's."

Gloria smiled and refocused her attention on her crossword puzzle. "Good."

"Good? I thought you didn't like her."

She looked surprised. "I never said that."

"But you said..."

"I said a lot of stupid things. I thought the timing was off... and it is, but you've been moping around here for weeks like a dog that's lost his prized bone and I'm tired of it. If you love her, you should tell her so."

Declan took a step and pressed his back against the wall. "I'm too young."

"Yep," Gloria said with a smile. She scrawled a few clumsy letters on her crossword puzzle. "Like I said, the timing is off, but what are you going to do?"

"I could stay away from her."

Gloria tapped the eraser end of her pencil on the table. "That's not really working."

Declan lifted his chin. "It could work."

"Hmm... maybe if you were going to Duke, but even then I think you'd be miserable. You were much better with her than you've been without her."

Declan bit his lip and looked out the window. "What if she doesn't feel the same? What if she's better off without me?"

"She should at least be given the choice, don't you think?" Gloria waved her pencil at him. "Get out of here. Don't talk yourself out of it. If you let her go without saying something, you'll be moping around here for the rest of your life."

Declan didn't move.

Gloria narrowed her eyes and lowered her voice. "Don't you make me throw you out!"

Declan laughed. "You can't."

"Don't try me," she growled. "Man-up! Tell her how you feel!"

Declan found Lizbet dragging a tarp across the yard. She wore cut-off jeans, a bikini top, and a pair of red plastic flip-flops. She had a strange pair of goggles on her head and a rifle strapped to her back.

She froze when she saw him, and an expression he couldn't read flashed across her face. When she didn't point the gun at him, he took that as a good sign and climbed from the car.

"Hey," he said. "There's something I have to tell you."

She glanced at the sun as if trying to read it. "I'm the one who needs to tell you something."

"Okay, you first."

"I'm sorry I stood you up."

He dipped his head. "I'm sorry, too."

"For what?"

"For ruining things between us." He closed the gap between them. "I'm miserable without you."

A smile flitted across her face. "I'm miserable without you, too." She picked up his hands and drew them to her lips. "I love you, but can we talk about this tomorrow?"

He rocked back on his feet. "No. I have to talk about this now."

"Now?" Her voice squeaked. "I can't talk right now."

"Why not? What are you doing?"

"I can't tell you."

A large crow flew overhead, squawking.

Lizbet frowned at it before turning back to him. She threw her arms around him, went to her tiptoes, and planted a kiss on his chin. "Tomorrow," she promised before turning away, picking up her tarp, and striding across the driveway, ducking under the fence, and striding through the pasture.

Declan watched her, frowning. What had just happened? This was not how it was supposed to go. She'd told him she loved him, but then she'd left. Why? Was she planning on staying the night—again—with Matias? She wouldn't do that, would she? She couldn't think he'd be okay with that, right?

He battled indecision for a moment, then he marched after her. He caught up to her at the edge of the woods. She'd lost the tarp somewhere. He was just about to speak up, when he noticed a fox sitting directly opposite her. It didn't even flinch when she knelt beside him. Rustling in the woods drew his attention. He jumped behind a tree when he spotted a bear. He started to call out to warn Lizbet, but stopped when she began to speak.

"I'm so honored that you would join us," she said to the bear.

The creature as huge as a refrigerator ambled toward her and roared.

Declan sucked in a deep breath and his knees buckled. To his amazement, Lizbet just smiled and looked pleased.

"Your help means a lot," she said. "Let's wait a few minutes for the others to join us."

Declan leaned against the tree with weak knees. Who were the others? Was she expecting opossum? Maybe a deer or two? Seconds after the thought crossed his mind, a herd of deer appeared, and raccoons gathered in the trees, sharing space with squirrels, opossum, and chipmunks. A flock of crows gathered overhead and cows and horses trampled across the pasture. The creatures assembled around Lizbet.

Lizbet addressed the crowd. "I really appreciate your willingness to put aside your animosity to fight our common enemy. As you know, a pack of wolves has been terrorizing our community. There have even been some deaths."

Chattering, growling, and murmuring rippled through the crowd.

"It needs to stop," Lizbet said. "And I believe it can. But only if we all work together."

A crow fluttered to perch on Lizbet's shoulder. It whispered in her ear and she stopped and slowly turned in Declan's direction. He thought about hiding, but realized he could never do so from the birds.

"What are you doing here, Declan?" she asked, her voice hard.

He stepped out from behind the tree, amazed to find he was almost as scared of Lizbet as he was of the bear. "What—" His voice cracked. He cleared his throat and tried again. "What are you doing?"

She twisted her lips together and scowled at him. He could tell she was battling between the truth and a lie. Finally, she said, "I'm going to catch a werewolf."

Regard heaven as your father,
earth as your mother and all things
as your brothers and sisters.
~Tribe Unknown

Chapter Sixteen

You need to go," she said, bristling. "This is going to be dangerous."

"I'm staying." He puffed out his chest like a rooster preparing for battle, which almost made her smile. It would have if the situation wasn't so dire.

"I'm serious, you have to leave." Lizbet put her hand on his chest to keep him away.

Declan stepped closer but froze when the bear made a low, threatening sound in the back of his throat.

Lizbet's smile was apologetic. "We have you just a little outnumbered."

"I don't understand any of this."

"I wouldn't expect you to."

"These animals... they listen to you."

She gave him a small nod. "They listen to you, too."

"But they don't do what I say."

"Why should they? Do you do what they say?"

"How can I know what they say? How can you?"

She shrugged. "I don't know. But I understand them and they understand me. I help them and they help me. Within reason."

"Tell one of them to do something."

She glanced at the sky. The sun had turned into a pink puddle on the horizon. "I will not. They're not circus ponies."

"I'm not really sure I'm buying this."

She smirked. "Really?" She looked to the sky. "Get him out of here," she said to the crows.

The crows formed a black shuttering cloud in the darkening sky. They swooped and cawed, happy to oblige. They dove at Declan's head.

"Yah!" He put both arms over his head and cowered. "Call them off!"

"Okay, guys, don't hurt him."

"But you said!"

"I know. I just wanted to scare him." Lizbet put her hands on her hips. "Will you go now?"

Declan uncovered his head and glanced up at the birds circling above. It looked as if he had his own personal bird-tornado. He sat down.

"Fine, you can stay, the rest of us are leaving." Lizbet jerked her thumb over her shoulder. "This way, everyone." She pointed at a large buck with an impressive set of antlers. "Elroy, make sure he doesn't get hurt."

Elroy stepped forward, shook his massive antlers at Declan and snorted.

Declan held up his hands to ward off the buck. Lizbet felt a wave of compassion for him. She edged herself between Elroy and Declan and took Declan's hand. "I can't even imagine how surprising and overwhelming this must be for you."

"Do you think?"

She laid her open palm on his cheek. "This is who I am. I'm the girl who can talk to animals but who also happens to be in love with you."

"You talk to animals and you chase werewolves. What about vampires?"

"No such thing."

"How do you know?"

She stooped to brush her lips against his. "I don't have time to argue with you. The moon will rise soon."

"Full moon?"

She nodded.

"This wolf. Is it the same animal that attacked my grandfather?"

"Probably, but I can't be sure."

"Then shouldn't I be the one to kill him?"

"No."

"Why not?"

"Well, for one thing, I'm a better shot and for another, I have a bear on my side."

Declan studied the bear. "Good point."

She turned to leave. "Stay here with Elroy. You'll be safer in the pasture than in the woods."

The crows fluttered above her, cocky and confident in their ability to escape the wolf in a way the earthbound animals could never be. Lizbet tossed one of the ropes to one bird who caught it in his beak and draped it over a tree branch. Lizbet caught the end of it and tied it to the antlers of a buck. The deer trembled with fear, but he remained still. Lizbet whispered to him as she worked the knots. "This will all be over soon. We'll be safer when he's gone. You'll be a hero."

She repeated the process with each rope tied to each corner of the tarp before covering the tarp with branches and fallen leaves. Then she waited. The animals gathered around her, anticipation and fear radiating from them. Their peculiar stillness should have sent the wolf a warning, but assured of his own power, the creature burst into the night.

He flew at Lizbet and landed where she'd stood only seconds before.

"Now!" she cried.

The deer ran in opposite directions, lifting the tarp and

then capturing the wolf in the air. His claws shredded the tarp and his growls and snarls filled the night air. Lizbet raised the gun to shoot.

But she couldn't do it.

She reminded herself of the torn and bloody sheep. She recalled what he'd done to Declan's grandfather and the nurse. Still, the gun wavered.

He was a creature.

Beautiful.

Terrifying.

Driven by hunger and passion she didn't share, but she could understand.

Beside her, the bear growled. She owed the animals this. They had placed their lives and their trust in her.

Raising the barrel of the long gun at the writhing tarp, she fired.

The creature howled. His cries drowned out all other sounds. She'd wounded him, but hadn't killed him. The shredded tarp gave way, and the wolf fell to the forest floor. He leaped toward Lizbet, but the bear cuffed him in the head, sending him rolling in the dirt. The wolf sprang to his feet and bounded out of sight. Lizbet took off after him, her animal posse running beside her.

A cry rang out.

"Declan!" she screamed, and ran faster.

In the clearing, a thrashing, naked Leo Cabriolet lay at Declan's feet.

"The lawyer?" Lizbet's words came out in huffs as she reached Declan.

Cabriolet whimpered and clutched at his heart.

"You shot him," Declan said.

"He was a wolf."

Declan shook his head. "I don't think that's going to hold up in a court of law."

"Leave him with me. Men will never find him," the bear said. He picked up the attorney, threw him over his shoulder and ambled away.

"What's going to happen to him?" Declan asked.

Lizbet shook her head. "I'm not sure." She reached for Declan, but he winced at her touch. She noticed his bloody hand. "What happened to you?"

Declan held up his hand and wrapped it in the end of his T-shirt. "It's nothing."

"Let's put something on it so it won't get infected."

He turned to her and pulled her close. "I don't want to think about it right now."

"What do you want to do?"

He growled before he kissed her. Pulling away, he rested his forehead on hers. "I have so many questions."

"I don't have all the answers."

"You have more than I do."

She lifted a shoulder and grinned. "Maybe."

"If anyone had to be a werewolf," Declan said, "I really wanted it to be Godwin."

"I know, right?"

"My mom... why does she always fall for monsters?"

"Should we go ask her?"

"I don't want to think about my mom right now," Declan said right before he kissed her again.

He tucked her hand into his pocket and walked her across the pasture to the farmhouse backdoor. "See you tomorrow?"

She nodded.

"Let's work out our schedules for school," he said.

"You're going to go to the UW?"

He nodded.

She squeezed his hand. "It's a good plan."

He dropped another light kiss on her lips. "See you tomorrow."

Inside her room, Lizbet slid off her clothes and stepped into her pajamas. After brushing her teeth, she paused by the window. Declan's car still stood in the driveway.

Odd.

She didn't see him in the driver's seat. She scanned the shadowy woods, but didn't see him there, either. Maybe the car's battery had died. Or it was out of gas. Or... She shook herself.

It had been a traumatic night. She needed to decompress. After switching off her light, she settled into bed, wishing that sleep could overtake her. But her mind roiled with questions. Leo Cabriolet was a werewolf. The bear had taken care of him, but what about Godwin? She suspected he was also a werewolf and had been involved in Gloria's accident. She thought about how she could lay another trap and as she schemed she began to drift into sleep.

To touch the earth is
to have harmony with nature.
~Oglala Sioux

Chapter Seventeen

Silence had its own music. Amplified, a void sucking in all the sounds that should have been: chattering squirrels, calling birds, the buzz of insects. Still. Dark. Silence as heavy as water.

Hunger burned the back of his throat and tightened his gut. He padded across the forest floor. A carpeting of pine needles and soft soil muffled his footfalls. Above the trees' canopy, a smattering of stars glistened, pale against a cloud-filled night. Mist shrouded the round, full strawberry moon.

He sat back on his haunches and lifted his head toward the moon. Snatches of conversations drifted by. *The girl did this...Yes, he's dead...revenge will be bittersweet...because she is your child?*

His ears twitched. The voices... they belonged to the wind. Or did they? Who was the girl spoken of? Could it be Lizbet?

Her name sent ripples of apprehension through his blood. He gazed at his paw... so foreign. How had he transformed into this creature? Standing on all fours, he loped through the woods aimlessly, fighting the hunger that zinged through his veins. He came to a clearing at the top of a hill and shuddered to a stop in a circle of stones. This place... Lizbet had told him of this place.

Again, her name sent a shiver of dread down his spine. Those voices on the wind... they meant Lizbet harm. Could he protect her better as a wolf or as a man? He turned and ran.

His agility amazed him. He tore through the woods at lightning speed, the trees flashing by, his paws barely even touching the ground. Power surged through his flanks. A feeling of invincibility coursed through him. Moments later he paused beneath the tree beside the farmhouse and gazed up at Lizbet's window, willing her to join him in the moonlight. He called her name, but all that came out was a whimper.

The End

About Kristy Tate

USA Today bestselling author Kristy Tate--writing her own happily-ever-after one day (and sentence) at a time.

She's the author of more than twenty books, including the bestselling and award-winning Beyond Series and the Kindle Scout winning Witch Ways series. She writes mysteries with romance, humorous romance, light-hearted young adult romance, and urban fantasy.

When she's not reading, writing, or traveling, she can be found playing games with her family, hiking with her dogs, or watching movies while eating brownies.

Turn the page and enjoy a
sneak peek at Melee,
Book 3 in the
Menagerie Series

It is during the wee hours when our
most immense dreams come to us.
—Jean Arp
From Lizbet's Studies

Chapter One

As sunlight touched the eastern sky Declan sat up, shivering. Brushing twigs and leaves off his naked skin, he crawled to huddle behind a huckleberry bush to make sense of things. His whole world tilted as he tried to process what had happened. He had spent the night in the woods. Naked?

How could he have forgotten something as important as his clothes?

Beyond the woods, Lizbet's house.

Only the barn stirred with life. Horses nickered, goats bleated, pigs snorted—all were waiting for their breakfast, and Declan knew who would provide it. Lizbet. He couldn't face her. Not like this. After shooting a quick glance at the house, wondering if anyone was awake to witness his streaking, he ran for his car.

The keys. Where were they? In the pocket of his jeans. But where were his pants? Crouching behind the Mercedes, he spotted them—or what was left of them—at the edge of the woods. He commando crawled through the tall grass, snake-like, flinching as twigs and pebbles poked and pierced his skin. All his clothes had been ripped to shreds, but thankfully, his keys were still in the remains of his pocket. He scooped up the cottony threads of what had once been his clothes.

His shivering accelerated as he pressed the key fob, crawled back through the grass, avoiding anything sharp or dangerous looking, and lifted the car's door handle. Inside the Mercedes, he started the engine and turned up the heater full blast. He glanced in the rearview mirror, half expecting to see a furry snout instead of his nose and unshaved chin. He looked exactly like himself, but... he gazed at his arms and chest... different. He studied the wolf bite on his hand. A few hours ago the puncture wounds had been a bloody mess, but it had since healed to a pink line. Strange.

By the time he arrived at his grandfather's house in the University District, he had practically convinced himself that it had all been a bad dream.

But his shredded clothes told a different story.

He collapsed onto his bed just after dawn and fell into a restless sleep.

Lizbet addressed a crowd of gathered animals. "I really appreciate your willingness to put aside your animosity to fight our common enemy. As you know, a pack of wolves has been terrorizing our community. There have even been some deaths."

Chattering, growling, and murmuring rippled through the crowd.

"It needs to stop," Lizbet said. "And I believe it can. But only if we all work together."

A crow fluttered to perch on Lizbet's shoulder. It whispered in her ear and she stopped and slowly turned in Declan's direction. He thought about hiding, but realized he could never do so from the birds.

"What are you doing here, Declan?" she asked, her voice hard.

He stepped out from behind the tree, amazed to find he was almost as scared of Lizbet as he was of the bear. "What—" His voice cracked. He cleared his throat and tried again. "What are you doing?"

She twisted her lips together and scowled at him. He could tell she was battling between the truth and a lie. Finally, she said, "I'm going to catch a werewolf."

Drenched in sweat, Declan bolted up, kicking the covers off. He swung his legs off the side of the bed and sat with his elbows on his knees and his head in his hands. He willed his heart to stop racing. It's only a dream, he

told himself. But it was more than that. It was a memory. A painful one.

And if it was a memory, it meant that the other, more terrifying dreams could also be memories. He padded over to his computer, sat down in front of it, and turned it on. He typed "night terrors" into the search engine.

> *Episodes usually occur 1 to 2 hours after going to sleep and can last from 1 to 30 minutes. The victim will look like himself with open eyes but his expression will be vacant, if not horror-struck. Waking a victim will prove difficult, if not impossible. Upon waking, he or she won't remember the incident, no matter what terror he has endured.*
>
> *During an episode, it is typical for one to exhibit intense fear or agitation. They may be violent. They will not be cognizant of their surroundings. Their breathing may quicken and their heartrate increase. They may perspire profusely. They may scream and try to fight demons that only they can see.*
>
> *Night terrors are different from nightmares. Nightmares are frightening dreams that can often be recalled the next morning in vivid detail. Night terrors leave no trace in the memory.*

That was it. Night terrors. Although, according to this article, victims of night terrors were usually under the age of twelve. But Declan wrote off his experience in the woods as night terrors—a phenomenon brought on by the shock

of Lizbet's revelations. For that, of course, he couldn't manufacture a rational explanation without engaging in a losing argument with her—and maybe a bear or a skunk. No sense in picking a fight he had no chance of winning. But as for his own personal nightmare—he didn't need to revisit it.

He hoped.

It was only a little after six. He could sleep for another couple of hours. But could and would were two very different concepts. Silently, he crept from his room and down the hall and peeked through his mom's ajar bedroom door. She slept curled in a ball in the middle of her king-size bed, the bedclothes wrapped around her legs, her arms tucked under her. He tiptoed across the long stretch of carpet, passing through a swath of early morning light streaming through the window. In her bathroom, he found her collection of medicine in the cabinet. He grabbed four bottles, and after another glance at his mom, he took them into her closet and closed the door before flipping on the light.

The sudden brightness stung his eyes. It took a moment for his vision to clear. Surrounded by his mom's power suits, silky dresses, and shoes, he scanned the medicine labels before selecting the one that read, For relief of sleeplessness when associated with pain.

He knew what he was doing was wrong, but he rationalized away his guilt. He told himself emotional pain was just as real as physical pain. He swallowed the pills dry.

Elizabeth stood in the far corner of her garden waving her cane at a flock of sparrows.

"Something wrong, Grandma?" Lizbet asked, coming up behind her.

"These dad-gum birds are eating all of my grapes!" Elizabeth groused.

"They have to feed their families, too," Lizbet said gently as she eyed the small, hard green balls that had weeks to go before being palatable to anyone other than the sparrows.

Elizabeth blew out a sigh. "You sound like you're on their side!"

"I didn't know there were any sides," Lizbet said. "I'm just pointing out—"

"Ugh. You sound like Josie!" Elizabeth sloshed through the muddy garden patch. "She's always trying to get me to sell this place."

That was not only unfair, it was also untrue. "I don't want you to sell the ranch, and I know my mom doesn't either."

Elizabeth sniffed as she moved between the corn stalks. Some had already grown past her shoulders while others barely reached her waist. A few of the taller stalks had baby ears of corn and sported puffs of silk.

"This place is my life," Elizabeth said. "I wouldn't know what to do with myself if I had to vegetate in Josie's condo all day."

Lizbet trailed after her grandmother. Because she was a good five inches shorter than her grandmother, some of the stalks touched her hair and threatened to poke her in the eye with their floppy leaves. "No one is asking you to move in with Josie."

Elizabeth made a harrumphing sound. "We're going to have to make some salsa out of these tomatoes," she said. "If we can keep the deer out of here."

Lizbet took note of the hundreds of nearly ripe tomatoes. Only a few, that she could see, had deer bites in them. "I think the critters have shown a lot of self-restraint," Lizbet said.

Elizabeth turned and gave her an are-you-insane look.

"Come on, Grandma," Lizbet said, taking Elizabeth's arm. "Let's go and make some lunch."

When an invitation to Nicole's going away party coincided with the first night of August's full moon, only a niggle of warning flashed in the back of Declan's mind.

"Are you sure you want to go?" Declan asked Lizbet as they browsed the bookstore for used textbooks. He would be a freshman at the University of Washington at the end of September and Lizbet would start classes at Queen Anne Community College a couple of weeks before that.

"Sure, why not?" Lizbet flipped her curls over her shoulder and gave him a smile that sent him over the moon.

"Well, it's not as if you're friends..."

"But she's your friend, right?"

"Yeah, but..."

"Come on, it'll be good for me. I'm trying to be more social." She bumped him with her hip before moving down the aisle. She glanced at her list of required books for the upcoming semester.

"You're plenty social." Declan trailed after her, but stopped as a title caught his eye.

The Meaning and Translation of Dreams. He pulled it off the shelf and flipped it open.

People who are anxious or overtired are more likely to sleepwalk or experience sleep terrors. A relaxing routine paired with an early bedtime can help prevent sleep disturbances.

Avoid sleepwalking injuries by making the bedroom and house as safe as possible. Consider the following precautions:

Make sure there are no sharp or breakable objects near the bed.

Install gates on stairways.

Lock doors and windows.

If psychological stress contributes to disordered sleep, counseling may help. Both children and adults may benefit from hypnosis or biofeedback.

In some cases, a doctor may prescribe short-acting sleep

or antianxiety medications to reduce or eliminate episodes.

    Seek professional help if:

- *Episodes are frequent or severe.*
- *The sleepwalker gets injured during episodes.*
- *The sleepwalker leaves the house.*
- *Nighttime episodes are accompanied by daytime sleepiness.*
- *Stress, anxiety or other psychological factors may be contributing to sleep disturbances.*

Sleepwalkers occasionally injure themselves or others. But most episodes of sleepwalking and sleep terrors are brief and harmless.

Lizbet glanced over his shoulder. "What's this?"

He slammed the book shut. "Nothing."

"You having problems sleeping?"

"Not really. Just that one night." He slipped the book back onto the shelf.

"What night?" she pressed.

He shrugged her question off. "Listen. It makes sense. Talking animals, werewolves, and were-Schnauzers. Anyone would have nightmares. It was a lot to process." A sudden memory assaulted him and he closed his eyes, trying to tune it out.

    Hunger burned the back of his throat and tightened his gut. He padded across the forest floor. A carpeting of pine needles and soft soil muffled his footfalls. Above the trees' canopy, a smattering of stars glistened, pale against a cloud-filled night. Mist shrouded the round, full strawberry moon.

He sat back on his haunches and lifted his head toward the moon. Snatches of conversations drifted by. Apprehension surged through his blood. He gazed at his paw...so foreign. How had he transformed into this creature? Standing on all fours, he loped through the woods aimlessly, fighting the hunger that zinged through his veins.

"Of course." Lizbet looped her arm around his and pulled him into a sideways hug and out of the memory. Hallucination. Nightmare... whatever it was.

"It's amazing that we're both not bonkers," she said.

"Bonkers," he murmured. His gaze landed on another book, *Mental Health for Dummies.*

He needed help.

Music thrummed through the open windows. Someone had hung a disco ball from the dining room chandelier and shafts of multicolored light sparkled on the dark lawn. Kids in jeans, T-shirts, and UW hoodies lounged on the front porch. Lizbet wanted to belong, but she still felt like a poser. This was Declan's world, as foreign to her as the moon.

She picked out Baxter, Declan's oversized friend, Maria, her neighbor, and McNally, another teammate of Declan's from East End High's basketball team all standing in a tight

circle just inside the double-wide doors. She tightened her grip on Declan's hand.

He wore blue jeans, flip-flops, and a Twenty One Pilots T-shirt. Trying to fit in, she'd chosen a nearly identical outfit, but her T-shirt and jeans couldn't hide her curves... and nothing could tame her curls.

As if sensing her insecurity, Declan dropped a quick kiss on her temple.

"Who's that with Nicole?" she asked, nodding at a guy with a Cross-Fitter's build leaning against the porch railing, his eyes trained on Nicole, a lithe blonde with flushed cheeks.

"Jason Norbit. Her old squeeze. They broke up a while ago."

"You mean when she applied to Duke?"

Declan dipped his chin. "He's going to UW on a football scholarship."

Lizbet bit her bottom lip as she followed Declan up the porch steps and through the doorway. She had her own theories about why Nicole had applied to Duke.

Nicole was beautiful in an ice-queen way. Her home had the same understated elegance—the disco ball being the notable exception. Someone had carried the dining room table out through the French doors to the back patio and people danced on the hardwood floor beneath the spinning lights.

"Want to dance?" Declan asked.

"No." The thought horrified her. She'd never danced

before in front of a crowd. Her thoughts flitted back to the first time she had ever danced... with Declan... in the moonlight. Dancing had turned to kissing. That had been a first for her, too. "Do you?"

He shook his head, grinned as if he shared her memories, and put his hand on her shoulder to steer her outside to his cluster of friends surrounding the food-piled dining room table.

Nicole waylaid them. "Hey, Declan. Any second thoughts about ditching Duke?"

Declan shook his head. "Sorry, Nicki, you're on your own."

Jason pulled himself away from the wall and draped his arm across Nicole's shoulder. "Not quite on her own. There's only about three thousand in the freshman class."

Lizbet wasn't sure, but she thought she saw a flicker of irritation in Nicole's eyes.

McNally appeared at Declan's side and elbowed him. "Yeah, now that you're going to UW, have you thought about playing intermural basketball?"

"Basketball?" A girl Lizbet didn't know broke into the conversation. "That's no fun. What about ultimate frisbee?" She flashed Declan a smile full of perfectly straight, bright white teeth. "That's co-ed."

"How about you?" Jason nodded at Lizbet. "Where you headed?"

"Queen Anne Community," Lizbet said. "Staying local."

Jason's gaze swept over her and lingered on her lips.

"Me, too." He lifted his soda bottle as if to clink her invisible goblet in a toast.

Lizbet sent Declan a quick glance, but he was lost in conversation with McNally and the unknown girl, debating the virtues of basketball and ultimate frisbee.

Jason leaned forward, placing his hand on the wall directly behind Lizbet and making her feel pinned. "What's your story?"

Lizbet knew he wouldn't believe her if she were stupid enough to tell him. She tested him. "Well, last month I killed a werewolf. How about you?"

He laughed as if she were joking. "So you're like Buffy? A vampire slayer?"

"No vampires," she said in all seriousness. "I tend to stick to creatures."

He nodded and a glint she didn't like filled his eyes.

"Seriously," she said. "I'm auditing a mythology class from Professor Madison at the University of Washington right now."

"What are you going to do with that? Kill more werewolves?"

"I'd rather just scare them away."

He snorted. "You're a tiny thing. It's hard to believe you could scare anything."

She blinked at him. "You'd be surprised."

"You're like a werewolf warrior?"

She wanted to smile to show him his invasion of her

personal space wasn't making her crazy, but the closer Jason pressed, the more uncomfortable she felt. She looked over his shoulder for Declan, but couldn't see him. Everyone else had deserted the porch and gone inside. Annoyance flashed through her. She spotted a cat sitting on the windowsill, watching them with slit eyes. She crooked a finger at the animal. He responded by twitching his whiskers.

Jason flicked a glance over his shoulder before turning back to Lizbet. The cat stood, arched his back, and batted a dead moth out of the corner of the window toward Jason's crotch. Surprised, Jason jumped out of the line of fire.

Lizbet's lips twitched as she escaped. "Thanks," she whispered to the cat as she went to find Declan. She didn't see him with his friends in the backyard, in the mass of kids huddled in the kitchen, or in any of the circles of conversation in the living room. She thought she heard his laughter floating up the stairwell that led to the basement, but before she climbed halfway down, someone turned off the lights and plunged the basement into inky darkness.

"Everyone close your eyes," a girl said.

Lizbet froze on the stairs, unsure where to go or what to do. She risked tripping in the dark in either direction.

"Vampire, open your eyes and select your victim." Someone switched on a flashlight and a girl giggled.

Lizbet hurried down the stairs.

"Stop! Intruder!" Someone turned on the overhead light amidst groans.

Lizbet swallowed hard, suddenly aware that somehow she'd inadvertently pooped on the party.

The girl who seemed to be in charge pointed at Lizbet. "State your name and business." She had a severe haircut and wore I-mean-business glasses, a black turtleneck despite the warm summer night, and a pair of painted-on jeans.

"She's Lizbet and she's with me." Jason came up behind her and placed a heavy hand on her shoulder. "'Scuse us for interrupting. Mind if we join you?"

A couple of people made groaning sounds, but most murmured a welcome. The lights were doused before Lizbet even got a look around the room to see if Declan was in the crowd.

Jason tugged at her hand and she fell into a cross-legged position beside him. "I don't know this game," she whispered as she disentangled her fingers.

"It's easy. You'll catch on." Jason's warm breath fanned against her cheek. "As a werewolf warrior, you'll be a natural."

In the darkness, he seemed closer than she would have guessed. She inched away from him and bumped someone next to her. "Sorry," she hissed and held herself very still so as not to touch anyone else.

"Night has fallen... again," the game-master girl began. "While the villagers sleep, the vampire works the wages of death. Vampire, open your eyes and select your victim."

"Keep your eyes closed," Jason whispered, and he squeezed Lizbet's knee.

Moments later, the game-master girl flipped on a flashlight. "Everyone open your eyes." She flicked the flashlight at the faces of the twenty or so kids seated on the basement rug. When Lizbet saw Declan wasn't in their number, she wanted to leave, but she'd already interrupted the game once and didn't want to do it again.

"In the dark of night, a vampire stole into the home at twenty-eight Reynolds."

"Yeah! That's my house!" a redheaded kid with a smattering of freckles said.

The game-master girl slid him the evil eye. "While Carl slept, the vampire sucked his blood and left his lifeless body on the library floor."

"I have a library. Cool," Carl said.

"Yeah, like that's going to do you any good seeing as how you don't read," someone said.

"Hush!" a girl in a vintage Van Halen T-shirt hissed.

"You can't talk," a guy with hair like a hedgehog said. "You're dead."

Carl looked as if he wanted to argue, but he bit his tongue.

"I'm not sure I want to play this game," Lizbet whispered to Jason.

"You better be quiet, or else the vampire will kill you, too," Jason whispered.

"I'd be okay with that," Lizbet returned, "seeing as how I don't want to play."

"Silence!" the game-master girl called out. "Villagers, who among you executed this dastardly deed?" she asked as she flashed the light into the blinking faces of her friends. "Who is the vampire?"

Speculations and laughter flew. Lizbet tried to be a good sport, but with Jason's thigh pressing against hers, she felt increasingly uncomfortable. The guy sitting on her other side had excessive arm and leg hair so that every time she bumped into him she felt like she was touching a fur ball. Plus, he had onion breath.

"Okay! New round!" The game-master girl stood and flipped on the overhead light, illuminating the orange shag carpet and plaid sofas pushed up against the wood-paneled walls. "Everyone turn in your cards."

Lizbet had missed something.

Declan, Baxter, and McNally followed by Nicole and a couple of girls trooped down the stairs.

"Hey, can we join in?" Baxter asked. Lizbet had observed that because Baxter was so big, people rarely told him no. The circle widened to let him in while Declan inserted himself next to Lizbet.

"What brought you down here?" Declan whispered in her ear.

"I was looking for you."

"Hmm, I was looking for you, too." He kissed her lightly on the lips.

"Not yet, Lamb."

"Sorry," Declan said, sounding not in the least repentant.

Nicole, who had wedged herself on the other side of Jason, rolled her eyes.

The game-master girl hit the lights. "Villagers, close your eyes! Night has fallen in the village of the doomed. While the villagers slumber, the vampire stalks his prey."

Someone dropped in front of Lizbet and planted a sloppy wet kiss on her lips. She struggled and pushed him off.

"Yeah! That's the game!" Jason said.

"Sorry, I..." Lizbet jumped to her feet. "I told you I didn't want to play." Embarrassed, she crawled over people in the dark until she found the stairs and felt her way out of the basement. In the kitchen, she realized that Declan had followed her.

More Books by Kristy Tate

The Tick-Tock Between You and Me
Dreaming of You and Me
A Ghost of a Second Chance: A Rose Arbor Book
The Secret of Hailey's Comments
The Cowboy Encounter
The Highwayman Incident
The Pirate Episode
Beyond the Hallow
Stuck with You
Grace in the Mirror
Stealing Mercy
Beyond the Pale
Beyond the Fortuneteller's Tent
Witch Wishes
Witch Winter
The Little White Christmas Lie
The Rhyme's Library
Baby Blue Christmas
Seadrift
Rewriting Rita
Losing Penny: A Rose Arbor Romance
Witch One
Witch Ways

Indie Artist Press | Brackettville, Texas